FINN
AND THE
CLOUD EATER

FINN
AND THE
CLOUD EATER

NATHAN MICHAEL MILLER

NOGGINNOSE
PRESS

Nogginnose Press
PO Box 96
Smithville, AR 72466 USA
nogginnose.com

To Danny.
Slay giants.

CONTENTS

Finn Disobeys ... 1

Finn Meets Fleet ... 6

Finn Meets the Cloud Eater ... 12

Finn Seeks Advice ... 17

Finn and Una ... 21

Finn Helps the Animals ... 26

The Castle of the Winds ... 30

Finn Meets the Winds ... 34

The Trials of the North Wind ... 39

A Short Rest ... 46

The Fight ... 50

Setting Out ... 55

The Run ... 59

The Giant's Hideout ... 63

Unexpected Friends ... 67

Finn Meets the Clouds ... 72

A Plan Is Hatched 76

A Riddle in the Dark 80

Back Into the Light 86

The Battle Begins 92

Iteoir Scamall, the Cloud Eater 98

The Journey of the Whip 104

Crack! 108

The Feast 112

Home Again 120

- *1* -

FINN DISOBEYS

"I will tell you about giants, my sons," said Grandfather. His voice was as old as river stones, though not as smooth.

Finn and his father and his father's father were sitting on the porch of their little cottage, watching the sunset. They lived in a small kingdom called Loft that was high up in the mountains, and their family had been shepherds as long as anyone could remember.

Finn tore his eyes from the scattered pink and orange clouds in the sky and looked at Grandfather.

Grandfather did not speak much these days, so Finn hung on to his every word.

"Giants are nasty creatures," said Grandfather. "They are strange, too. Clever, yet narrow-minded. Powerful, yet petty."

"Have you ever seen one?" said Finn.

"I believe I have," said Grandfather. "From far away."

"How tall was it?" asked Finn.

"Taller than any tree I've ever seen," said Grandfather.

Finn shivered, though he was not cold.

"Giants live in many places," said Grandfather. "They live in mountains. Hills. Lakes. Forests. Some people say they *are* the lakes and mountains." He rocked in his chair for a moment, and Finn and Father waited for him to speak again.

When he did not, Father scratched his head and cleared his throat. "There are many stories of such creatures, it is true," Father said in his low voice, which always reminded Finn of the rumble of heavy wagons. "Why do you tell us this now? What brought it to your mind?"

Grandfather was silent for so long that Finn thought he had drifted to sleep, but his eyes were still wide open and reflected the red sunset.

"I was troubled by dreams," said Grandfather at last. "Strange dreams. Dreams about the Scáthán.[1] I felt I needed to warn you about the dangers of giants. Be careful, my sons, and do not trespass on their territory."

----

1 Pronounced 'SKA-han.'

"The Scáthán? That's the lake just beyond our fields, right?" said Finn. "We never bring our sheep to drink there. I've always wondered why."

"That's right," said Father. He turned in his chair and looked right into Finn's eyes. "I have never liked the feel of the lake myself. That is why I always tell you not to go to the Scáthán. No swimming. No playing in the water. No skipping rocks." Father ruffled Finn's hair.

"Yes sir," said Finn. And that was all they said about giants.

Finn had a hard time falling asleep that night, thinking about the forbidden lake. When he did, giants taller than trees filled his dreams.

. . . .

The next day, as they were letting the sheep out of the barn, Finn offered to take the sheep to the meadow to graze.

"You may," said Father. "I must mend our flock's shelter. It was damaged by the wind last night." He looked deep into Finn's eyes when he said this. "A shepherd tends to his flock, my son. You must take this job very seriously. Keep your eye on your flock, and do not wander off."

Finn swallowed. "Yes sir," he said.

He hoped his voice sounded normal. He hoped Father did not suspect what he was about to do.

Finn led the sheep to the farthest field. He chose this field for two reasons. The first was that it was out of sight from the house. Father, working on the shelter, would not see him; nor would Grandfather. The second reason Finn chose this field was that it was close to the Scáthán.

He watched the flock settle down and begin grazing in the field. After a while, Finn glanced in the direction of the house. He could not see anyone, which meant no one could see him.

He took a deep breath and slipped away from his flock. He had to be quiet and quick, or the sheep would notice him leaving and follow him. He passed through a handful of trees and bushes that separated their land from the lake. In a moment, he was on the shore of the Scáthán. He looked back, and could just barely make out a few sheep past the trees. Then he faced the lake.

The Scáthán's bright, cold water reflected the clouds above it like a huge mirror. Finn imagined a giant looking into the surface of the mirror and combing its hair or checking its teeth. He shook his head and made his way toward a tall bank ringed with reeds.

He stopped on the bank and held his breath. A mixture of fear and excitement made his heart pound. Surely the lake was the territory of a giant.

What had Grandfather said? That giants can live in lakes? A voice in the back of his head reminded him of his father's command to keep close watch over his sheep, but he pushed it away.

He leaned out over the water and looked into it. No giant. Finn could only see the blue sky behind the reflection of his head in the lake.

But was that his head?

For when he looked in the water, he knew something was not quite right. Was he really that tall? Was his hair that blonde—almost white? Finn gripped a handful of reeds at the edge of the water and leaned down towards his reflection to get a better look.

Baa-a-a-a-a!

A sheep bleated behind Finn, startling him. Finn turned his head quickly and saw a sheep standing behind him, chewing a mouthful of grass. It must have seen him sneak away and had followed him to the edge of the water.

Finn was already leaning too far over the water, and jerking his head around made him lose his balance. Finn's feet slipped off the edge of the bank and the reeds tore out of his hands.

As he fell, he closed his eyes and mouth and waited to splash into the water and feel its icy touch.

But there was no splash. And he felt no water.

– 2 –

FINN MEETS
FLEET

Finn had a horrible sensation that a hand with long, pointed fingernails was gripping the back of his neck and pulling him through a cold, dark, wet, narrow tunnel, like the tunnel of a worm. He kicked and yelled, trying to pull the hand off, but it held him firmly. Then the feeling became confused, and the clawed hand let go.

With a burst of light and a shock of water, Finn discovered that he was splashing in a lake. He looked around wildly for whatever had grabbed him, but saw nothing except for a nearby shore surrounded by reeds. He was breathing heavily and calming down when he heard a voice call from the bank.

"Hey, you! Where did you come from? Come on, this way."

The bank was high enough that Finn could not see the speaker, but he could see that a hand was reaching down to grab him. So he swam towards the bank. Before grabbing it, however, he treaded water and looked carefully at the hand that was reaching down to him. The fingernails were no longer than normal, and even seemed a bit chewed. This couldn't have been the hand that had seemed to grab him a moment ago.

"Are you going to take all day?" the voice said impatiently. "I could leave you down there if I wanted to." Finn reached up and took the hand. He was heaved up past the reeds and onto the bank.

"This is a strange fish. It looks like a little boy," the voice said. "Where did you come from? I didn't see you jump in."

Once Finn was on his feet, he had the chance to see who had helped him up the bank. A boy, not much older than himself, stood before him. Finn recognized the boy and his blonde hair.

"You!" Finn said. "I saw you when I looked in the water. And I'm *not* a little boy. You can't be much older than me."

"Actually," said the boy, "*I* saw *you* in the water. And I'm far older than you."

"What are you doing here?" said Finn. It annoyed him to be called a little boy by someone who could be no more than a year older than he was. This other boy had blonde hair, so blonde it was nearly white, and he wore a funny kind of tunic. He was holding a shepherd's crook.

"I'm watching my flock. That's it right over there," said the boy. He pointed at the lake shore.

"That's not your flock! That's my..." Finn started to say. But something was not quite right. The white shapes on the lake shore were not curly-haired like his own sheep. In fact, they looked quite different...

"Why, they're clouds!" said Finn.

"Of course they are," said the boy, surprised at Finn's surprise. "My name's Fleet; what's yours?"

"That's a funny name. I'm Finn."

"You're one to talk. 'Finn' is a funny name," said Fleet. "I'll ask again: what are you doing in my field?"

"But you don't shepherd clouds," said Finn. "What do they eat?"

Fleet sighed and rolled his eyes. "The dew from the grass, of course," he said. "Were you born under the moron star? Now for the last time, will you tell me what you're doing here?"

Finn hardly heard him.

Where was he? This place looked similar to home, but for two exceptions: the boy, and the flock of clouds grazing on the dew. Finn turned back to the Scáthán and looked in. He saw nothing but his own reflection, and...

"My sheep!" he said.

There in the reflection of the water, the wide eyes of a sheep looked at him. Finn looked back at Fleet. "I fell in the water of the lake, that's how I got here. It was an accident—sort of. Something grabbed me and pulled me through. Say, is there anyone else around here? Someone…someone with long fingernails?" said Finn.

Fleet raised his eyebrows. "It is just me here. I have not seen anyone else around the lake. Long fingernails?"

"Yes," said Finn.

"I think you have been out in the sun too long, O mysterious traveler through the lake."

Finn frowned. "You don't have to believe me. I know it happened. Anyway, I need to take care of my flock. I bet if I jump into the lake again, I will get through to the other side and be back home."

"Oh, I see. You're a shepherd too," said Fleet. He thought for a moment. "You might be crazy, but…must you go so soon? We've only just met."

Finn remembered what his father had told him that morning. *A shepherd protects his flock, Father had said, and you must take this job seriously.* Of course, Finn should have gone home right away.

But wouldn't the sheep be fine without him for a while?

"Fine," said Finn. "I'll stay. But answer one question first: are there any giants around here?"

"No...no," said Fleet. He glanced at the lake. "I don't think so, anyway."

Then Fleet told Finn to try to catch a cloud.

Finn ran after one as it drifted across the field, but when he tried to wrap his arms around it, he met nothing but icy air that shocked his lungs and drenched his hair. Fleet rolled around on the grass, laughing, while Finn shivered. The cloud floated away from Finn indignantly.

"Let's skip rocks in the lake. You go first," said Fleet with a sly grin.

"No," said Finn. "I don't think that's a good idea." He remembered what Grandfather had said about trespassing on a giant's territory, and how a giant would eat him, given the chance. Skipping stones on a giant's lake seemed foolish.

"What are you, scared?" said Fleet.

"No," said Finn. "Why don't you do it? Are you *sure* there are no giants around here?"

"Aha, I see. You were born under the scaredy-cat star," said Fleet.

That settled it.

Finn picked up a rock and threw it into the lake. It splashed and sank without skipping.

They found the best skipping stones—round, smooth, and flat. Fleet was once able to skip a stone six times. Finn, however, never got more than three.

After a while, things got more and more out of hand. They started finding the biggest stones to throw in the water to make the biggest splash.

Moments after heaving a huge rock into the water, Finn heard a strange sound.

It was like a whistle, or a pipe, which started low and ended lower. And although it was low, it was very, very loud.

It shook Finn's ribcage. The flock of clouds seemed agitated when they heard it. They grouped together and quivered.

Before Finn could ask Fleet if he heard it too, Fleet pointed at the lake. Finn watched two spouts of water—no, were they pillars of mist?—rise out of the lake. They went up and up before meeting together to form a torso, which broadened quickly to form a big pot-belly.

Finn looked up and up into the face of a giant—a giant made of clouds.

He was taller than the tallest tree Finn had ever seen.

— 8 —

FINN MEETS THE CLOUD EATER

Dark clouds formed around the giant's head and thunder rumbled. The wind picked up, whipping leaves and dirt in the air. Finn watched as the flock of clouds fought against the wind, trying not to be blown away. And all the while, the giant grinned in the middle of the darksome storm.

Finn again remembered how his father warned him about the lake and instructed him to protect his flock. At once, he felt guilty about breaking his father's rules.

"What should we do?" asked Fleet. He looked as terrified as Finn felt.

"Well, he isn't doing anything now, is he? Maybe he'll ignore us," said Finn.

But the giant did not ignore them.

Instead, a great rumbling, shaking sound came from its mouth. With a chill colder than a cloud, the boys knew that the giant was laughing. The misty giant crouched down in the lake, just as you would crouch down if you were to talk to a couple of ants.

He bent his great face down to the boys. He was not ugly, exactly, for his face was also made of clouds. But his nose was huge, his mouth a gaping hole, and his eyes flashed with red lightning.

"Look who wandered so far from home," the giant said. The boys shivered. The giant's breath smelled like iron, and the ground when rain starts to fall.

"I felt a boy come through the waters of my lake. And I heard a great raucous ruckus of stones cast into my still waters. And look: here are two children by my Scáthán. You are trespassing."

"Leave, giant," said Fleet. "You don't belong here!" He brandished his crook.

"Oh, but this is *my* lake, little ones. It is you who does not belong here. Hmm, what shall I do with you? I could crush you in an instant..." Then the giant stopped. He cocked his head to one side, as if listening to something. Finn felt a prickle on the back of his neck, reminding him of the clawed hand that had pulled him out of the water, and he shivered. On the very edge of his hearing, he thought he could hear a voice whispering—but perhaps he was imagining it. *Was something speaking to the giant?* Then the whispering and the prickling sensation stopped, and the giant spoke again.

"Hmm," the giant said, stroking his chin. "I *could* crush you in an instant…but I think I see a better way to punish you. See here, I am hungry, and you have brought me dinner!" He gestured to Fleet's flock of clouds. "I shall take them from you, and all the clouds from this land, every last one. You and everything you love shall dry up like a shallow puddle."

With this, the giant stood up. He cupped his hands to his mouth and blew into them. Out came the strange, low whistle that the boys heard before, but this time it was different. It was like a song—an old song, so old that the oldest person alive would not remember it.

The clouds shivered. The clouds quivered. Then they stayed still. They floated out over the water and toward the giant. Clouds streamed from all across the sky, to cluster around the giant. Soon, the air was so thick with clouds that the boys could scarcely see the giant.

"No!" said Fleet, but it was too late.

The clouds gathered around the giant's legs as he laughed again, turned away from the shore, and lurched off into the lake. He splashed his way through, with the clouds grouping around and getting under his feet like frightened dogs.

The boys watched him travel further and further across the lake until their eyes were strained and they could see him no longer.

Finn was embarrassed to see Fleet begin to cry.

"This is my fault," said Fleet. "I told my father I would watch the clouds and that I would not go to the lake, but I did. And now look at what happened. My poor clouds! He will eat them all."

Finn was sorrowful as well. He decided not to tell Fleet that his own father had told him not to go to the Scáthán, either.

Now Finn noticed that not only were Fleet's clouds gone, but every cloud in the sky had followed the giant. It began to feel hot; the sun shone brightly without the clouds.

"I'm sorry, I need to get back to my sheep," said Finn.

"Just go," said Fleet. "Leave me alone."

Finn walked back to the lake and looked down in the water. No sheep looked back at him this time. He looked back at Fleet, then leaped into the water.

This time, there was a great splash. Cold water flooded his eyes and nose. His feet hit the shallow bottom. He pushed off it and broke the surface of the water, gasping. He grabbed the bank and pulled himself up.

And there was Fleet, right where Finn had left him.

Confused, Finn looked back at the water. It had not worked. He was not back at his own mountain. He was trapped here.

– 4 –

FINN SEEKS
ADVICE

"**I** know someone we can ask for help," said Fleet.

The two boys sat at the edge of the lake, dipping their toes in the water and staring out across the lake.

"She lives in a strange land, where there is only one of everything," Fleet said. "She will know what to do. She can get you back home, and she can tell me how to get my clouds back. How about that?"

"What do you mean 'only one of everything?'" said Finn. "Does she have only one leg? Or only one eye? Does she only have one strand of hair on her head...?"

Fleet rolled his eyes. "No. She has one set of legs and one set of eyes. And the most beautiful hair you've ever seen. Don't you know anything? No, I mean, in the land there is only one of *everything*. There's only one tree, one lake, one chicken. One woman. Like I said, it is a strange land. But the woman there is very wise. She will tell us what to do. She'll tell you how to get home and I can finally be rid of you. Let's go."

They went down the mountain. Finn could at once see that this mountain was not exactly the same as his own, for it was much shorter than his home kingdom of Loft.

They went across a meadow at the base of the mountain, then through a forest, across a stream, and up toward hill-country. And all the time, Fleet would run fast, faster than Finn could run, and would not wait up even though Finn called out to him. Then, when he was just about to go over a hill or Finn was about to lose sight of him, Fleet would stop and examine a flower or an insect or a rock until Finn could catch up. And all the while, Fleet did not make conversation.

Finally, they reached a river. "This is called the Ceann Amhàin,"[2] said Fleet. "It means 'just one.' We will be going into the Lady's territory now. Let me do the talking."

So Finn and Fleet crossed the river. Fleet used his shepherd's crook to balance himself. Finn nearly fell, but Fleet managed to steady him in time.

---

2 Pronounced 'chyan AHmin.'

Fleet was right. This was a very strange land. Everything was just slightly...off, but it was hard to see exactly why.

"Why," said Finn, "there's only one tuft of grass!"

"Of course," said Fleet. "Didn't I say? One of everything."

"Except for the Lady's two eyes. And us. We're two boys," said Finn.

Fleet scowled at him. "I can't wait until you go home," he said.

They went on into the Lady's land, where there was only one of everything. Eventually, they came to a cottage, next to an apple tree. Below that tree, a lone chicken scratched at the ground.

"I will talk to her. You make like a rock and don't talk, and we can finally get you out of my hair," said Fleet.

Fleet knocked on the door—just once.

"Come in," a woman's voice said. Fleet opened the door and they both stepped inside.

The whole cottage was one room: there was a bed in the corner with a single pillow, a table in the middle with a single chair, and a hearth with only one burning log in it. In the chair sat a woman.

Although she lived in a strange land, she was very ordinary. She had dark red hair which swept over her shoulders and green eyes. Finn was worried that when she opened her mouth, she would only have one tooth, but when she began speaking, he saw that this was not the case.

"I am Una," the Lady said. "Welcome to my home. I believe I know why you are here. I am missing something of my own," she said. She looked directly at Finn. "My one little cloud, which rests above the hill, is missing. Do you know anything about this?"

"It wasn't our fault," Finn muttered.

Fleet elbowed him.

She looked at Fleet, smiling. He shuffled his feet.

"Tell me what happened and what you did," said Una. "It will be much easier if you tell me everything now, omitting nothing."

The boys told her the whole story: how Finn came through the lake, how Fleet had gone against his father's wishes and brought his flock of clouds to the Scáthán, how they had thrown rocks into the water and how the giant had come and whistled his low whistle and led the clouds away.

The Lady did not interrupt but listened intently, and all the boys could hear was the sighing of the wind and the chicken clucking outside.

But Finn did not tell Una that he had disobeyed his own father.

- *5* -

FINN AND UNA

"I see," said Una, when they had finished their story. "The giant now has the clouds—not only yours, but mine and the whole world's clouds. You have angered the giant by trespassing on his lake, and now the world is in anguish. Without clouds, there will be no protection from the sun, and no rain—nor snow, nor hail, nor anything which comes from clouds. Without protection, the earth will dry up and the land will be parched. Without rain, the grass and grain and all living things will perish for lack of water. You are at fault and you must take responsibility for your actions."

Fleet hung his head, but Finn's face reddened. "All this just because we went to a lake? That's not fair," said Finn.

Una looked at him, and he felt as if she were gazing right through him and into his deepest thoughts.

"All this," she said, turning to Fleet, "because you disobeyed. And that is no small matter."

Finn felt uncomfortable. Although Una was talking about Fleet failing to obey, he knew that he himself was guilty as well.

"Do not be downcast," continued Una. "You have confessed, and you are no longer at war with yourself. You may turn your gaze to what you must do now. The journey will be difficult, but I will guide you." She stood up from the table, and Finn was struck by how tall and graceful she was. She walked to a basket beside her bed and pulled out a ball of bright red yarn.

Holding it out to the boys, she said, "Take this. Roll it before you, and it will unravel. Follow it where it leads; it will guide you to the Castle of the Winds. You must ask them for help. The North, South, and West Winds are holding council now to discuss the absence of the clouds."

Fleet gulped. Finn, taking the ball of yarn, raised his eyebrow at him. But Fleet did not say anything in response.

Una continued, "With the help of the four Winds, you must slay the giant."

"Slay him?" said Fleet. "How can we possibly do that? He's huge. There are only two of us. And *he's* just a boy," he said, pointing at Finn. Finn tried to stomp on his foot, but Fleet moved his foot away too quickly.

"This giant is fearsome," said the Lady. "They call him Iteoir Scamall,[3] the 'Cloud Eater.' Remember this, for names are quite powerful. He can call up storms and command lightning. He is dangerous, but he is gluttonous. He has a fondness for riddles. Do not tell him your name; this would give him power against you. Remember this when you face him."

After she said this, she gave them food for their journey (one apple, one pear, one hardboiled egg, one lump of cheese, and one loaf of bread) and bid them goodbye.

Fleet walked outside, but before Finn could follow him, Una pulled him aside.

"Finn, I know you are hiding something from me. What is it?" Una said. Her piercing green eyes bore right through Finn.

Finn felt a lump in his throat. "No, I'm not," he said.

Una was not smiling now. "Do not make things worse by adding lying to your disobedience," she said.

Finn swallowed hard. "Yes. I lied. Father told me not to go to the lake, Scáthán, just like Fleet's father told him not to. But I did anyway. I didn't mean to stay, either, but Fleet wanted me to stay."

---

3 Pronounced 'IH tyohr SKA-muhl.'

The Lady shook her head. "Do not shift the blame, either," she said. "This weighs on your shoulders alone. Fleet has a part to play, but when you meet the Cloud Eater, *you* must slay him. This is your task, and yours alone. But take heart. You have the ball of string?"

Finn nodded and held it up.

"Do not stray from it," she said. "Follow it where it leads. When it reaches the end of its tether, it will transform. You will know what to do then. This will help you defeat the giant. Also, there is more to Fleet than your eyes can see. He will be able to help you in your final battle, but *you* must strike the last blow. I have one more gift for you…"

She took a silver ring off her finger and handed it to him. It was finely twisted so that it resembled a thin snake eating its own tail. "Put it on your finger. This ring will allow you to understand and speak to all kinds of creatures. When you complete your task, return it to me."

Finn thanked her and put the ring on his finger.

No sooner had he put it on than he heard a voice from outside the window. The little voice came from the lawn. He went to the door and opened it. Fleet was leaning against the wall outside, but it could not have been his voice.

Next to the door was a little hen scratching, and the voice came from it.

"Scratch, scratch, scratch!" the hen clucked. "Where are all the bugs this season? My poor feet are growing weary. I must eat so I can lay an egg for my mistress."

So Finn knew that the ring indeed gave him the power to understand animals.

Finn tossed the little ball of red yarn before them. The ball of yarn rolled, rolled, rolled along, past the tree and the lone chicken and up, up, up the little hill beside the cottage. The little ball of yarn became no smaller, like a normal ball of yarn would, but stayed the same size it had been when it started. It stopped at the top of the hill and waited for the boys to follow.

As they followed the yarn up the hill, Una raised her hand in blessing and called after them, "When you complete your task, you may return to your own land, Finn. Godspeed."

The boys waved goodbye and went over the hill. And so they left the land called Ceann Amhàin.

– 6 –

FINN HELPS
THE ANIMALS

Finn and Fleet followed the red yarn where it led. Now that they had a mission, the boys felt better about their situation.

"That yarn is not going the right way," said Fleet. "I know the way to the Winds. They're meeting in the castle of the West Wind."

"How do you know that?" said Finn.

"I just know," said Fleet. "That's where the Winds always meet. I know a better way."

"Una said to follow the yarn, so that's what we're going to do," said Finn.

Fleet frowned, but then he shrugged, and they went on their way.

They traveled for a while down a dusty path. It was a narrow and overgrown path, most likely one that was usually used by deer and other animals rather than humans. Just as they neared a line of trees, Finn stopped. The yarn rolled on for a moment and then paused.

"Can you hear something?" said Finn.

"What do you mean?" said Fleet.

"I think I heard a voice. It's faint, almost a whisper. Wait for a moment and let me listen," said Finn. He remembered the ring that Una had given him that allowed him to understand all kinds of animals.

The two boys stopped. Finn strained his ears. He heard a voice close to the ground and stooped to hear it.

A very small voice said, "Tramp, tramp, tramp! All humans do is walk on us. Can they not watch their feet? They tread on us all day without mercy!"

It was an ant queen. Finn noticed that there were ants all along the path that he and Fleet were following.

Fleet asked Finn, "What do you hear?"

Finn said, "I hear an ant queen, and she is concerned for her people that we step on. Let's walk off the path." Finn and Fleet moved off of the path and walked on the grass beside it, where there were no ants.

Finn heard the ant queen say, "Thank you, stranger. We will remember you—one good turn deserves another!"

So Finn gained the trust of the ant queen and her subjects.

A little further on, Finn stopped again.

"Do you hear something again?" said Fleet.

"I hear another voice," said Finn. "This is a much louder voice and it seems to be in pain. Follow me!"

Finn ran on, closely followed by Fleet. The yarn rolled in the direction of the voice as well. They came across an eagle which was stuck in a metal trap.

"Woe!" cried the eagle. "Woe! I have been caught, and my children will starve if I cannot get to them. If only these boys would help me escape!" The boys hesitated to help—the eagle was large and her talons sharp. But they decided that the eagle would understand they were here to help, and worked together to pull the metal teeth of the trap apart. The eagle struggled free, and thankfully, seemed unharmed.

"Thank you, strangers," said the eagle, turning her fierce eye toward them and nodding. "I will remember that you helped me. One good turn deserves another." And off she flew.

The yarn rolled on and on, down the path.

Before long, it ran by a small stream. Finn saw a glistening fish struggling among the reeds on the river bank, gasping for air. It was a beautiful fish, with a yellow body and red-brown speckles all along its back. It seemed to have swum up too far and could not get back in the water.

He heard the fish gasping, "I will die here! I cannot breathe this air. I must get back to the water." Finn at once ran up to the fish and put the prisoner back in the water.

"Thank you!" he heard the fish bubble up from the stream, already swimming away. "You have a king's heart, boy. Thank you for your help—I will not forget it. If you ever fall into trouble, I will help you. One good turn deserves another." With a final flash in the sunlight, the fish swam out of sight.

Now the ball of yarn—all the while rolling in front of them—changed directions. It turned straight west and continued on.

"Now, at last, we are going to the Castle of the Winds," said Fleet.

"The ball of yarn led us to those animals, and Una gave me the ring so I could understand them," said Finn. "We helped them, and now they may be able to help us."

"What could ants do to help? And a fish is trapped in the water. That eagle is probably long gone and back at its nest—they won't remember you."

Finn shrugged and said, "Even if they don't, I'm glad we could help them. Let's keep up with the yarn and follow where it leads us."

So the boys followed the red yarn. It still did not grow smaller as it unraveled, but left a long, long trail of yarn behind them. How could so much yarn be in such a small ball?

THE CASTLE
OF THE WINDS

It was not an easy journey for Finn and Fleet. Gravity seemed to affect the boys far more than it did the ball of yarn. They climbed over rocky places, where the yarn skipped and jumped without slowing down. They splashed through streams while the yarn simply rolled through them. It never sank. Even in muddy and swampy areas where the boys struggled to walk, the red yarn was easily visible and never got dirty.

The boys, on the other hand, were sweaty, muddy, and tired.

They did not come across any more animals that needed help, although Finn could hear birds calling to one another and bugs whispering to one another at his feet.

All the while, Finn thought about what the Lady had said: how it was his fault, and his responsibility to slay the giant. At times, he felt angry. Why was this *his* problem? It just was not fair to ask him to kill a giant. When he thought of this, he snapped at Fleet and Fleet snapped at him.

At other times, Finn was scared. He remembered the great Cloud Eater; how his eyes flashed with lightning, his low whistle, his gaping mouth. When he thought of these things, he was silent and did not speak to Fleet.

And at other times, Finn wondered who Fleet was. Una had told him that there was more to Fleet than he could see. What did she mean? When he thought of this, he tried to ask Fleet questions. But Fleet rarely answered them fully, or else he changed the subject.

Finn also thought of the winds and how he would convince them to help. He had never spoken to winds before. Would they look like people, or would he be speaking to the air?

And all the while, the sun beat down mercilessly, for there were no clouds in the sky.

All of this made the journey very miserable for the two boys.

As they traveled, they could see they were steadily heading west. They knew this because the setting sun was in their eyes. Finn hoped they would reach somewhere to stay for the night before it got too dark.

Just as he was thinking that they would have to sleep outside, Finn saw a castle on a hill not too far away. And the yarn was heading right towards it.

"Look!" he said. He rushed forward but Fleet stayed back.

"Listen…" said Fleet. He was looking at his feet. "I can't go any further. The Lady said we would meet the Winds. I can't meet them, I'm not welcome."

"What do you mean? Are they mad at you? What did you do?"

Fleet did not answer right away.

"I just can't," he said eventually. He stopped toeing the dirt and looked up at Finn. His expression was hard to read. "*You* need to convince them to help. Don't worry about me; I'll meet you back here when you're done. Good luck." With that, he ran away and disappeared into the darkening night.

"Fleet, wait!" said Finn. "We need to follow the yarn!"

But it was too late. Fleet was gone. Finn would have to face the Winds alone.

With a sinking heart, Finn walked up the hill.

What will I say to the Winds? he thought. *Why did Fleet run off? Are the Winds really so terrifying?*

But even though Finn wanted to run off as well, he followed the red yarn.

Up, up the hill he went, until he crossed a bridge spanning a moat and came to a large door of wood and iron. He took a deep breath. There was a knocker on the door, but it was too high up for him.

Finn felt something bump his leg and he jumped. He looked down to see the red ball of yarn bumping at his heels. It was nudging him to go forward.

"Don't rush me," said Finn.

The ball of yarn rolled over his foot and bumped against the door again. Finn squeezed his eyes shut.

Knock, knock, knock.

The only answer to his knock was the door creaking open. And so Finn and the ball of yarn entered the Castle of the Winds.

- ℰ -

FINN MEETS THE WINDS

Finn entered the castle to find a large room filled with people. At the front of the room were courtiers in strange and bright clothing. The men wore strange hats and long capes, while the ladies wore fine dresses. Men lining the room wore gleaming suits of armor and held long, ornate halberds that carried blue flags. At the back of the crowd stood a more somber, quieter group, whose clothing was less bright and who held their hats in their hands. These, thought Finn, must be the common folk.

The room was very loud, and everyone was talking and shouting at once. Finn craned his neck to try and see the front of the room, and could just barely make out a dais on which were four thrones. That was where he needed to go.

As he pushed his way through, he could start to hear what each person was saying.

"How will my crops grow without rain?" moaned one man with a red face.

"My animals ail for water," said a woman whose hair was tied with a brown cloth.

Finn's face burned with shame. These people were all here because he had angered the giant.

Since the room was so crowded, no one noticed Finn as he pushed his way through to the front of the crowd. Soon he had made his way past the commoners and was bumping into the well-dressed people at the front. One woman had a blue dress with a trailing skirt that was so huge that Finn felt like he was wading through water to get past her.

"There is no shade, and the earth is cracked for want of rain," he heard a woman in a white dress say.

Another man with a nasally voice and a hat that hung from his head like a golden fern said, "The sun is wreaking havoc on my vineyards. I will be lucky to get half my crop this year." Finn did not like the look of this man's face; his eyes were too pinched and his nose seemed permanently wrinkled.

Finally, Finn made his way to the front of the room.

Finn could see one huge throne in the middle of the dais occupied by a tall man in a blue tunic with gold trim. His hair was long, brown, and curled, and it hung down to his broad shoulders. He wore a crown on his head. He was stroking his beard with one hand and listening intently to the crowd.

Beside him, a woman sat wearing gentle green and a silver circlet. Her eyes were the brightest blue, but her smile looked weary as she surveyed the room.

On either side of these two were smaller thrones. One was empty. In the other sat a boy who looked just like...

"Fleet!" Finn cried out.

The boy sat up and stared at him. Finn could see at once that it was not Fleet. This boy was a little taller and his nose was flatter, and he was wearing a blue tunic like the man in the big throne. But this boy had the same white hair as Fleet.

"Who are you?" said the boy. The moment he spoke, the crowd grew silent but for a few whispers.

Finn tried to retreat into the crowd, but they pushed him out into the middle of the floor in front of the thrones. The crowd moved into the corners of the room so that Finn stood there alone, feeling very small.

"I ask again, boy, who are you to call me by my brother's name?" said the boy on the throne.

"My name is Finn."

"And do you not know who I am?" said the boy.

"I thought I did," said Finn, "but I see I am mistaken."

"That you are," said the boy, and was about to say more. But the king in the great throne—for a king he must be, with his crown of gold—raised his hand, and the boy fell silent.

"Finn," said the king, "you are not from this place, if you do not know who we are. Where do you hail from?"

The king's voice was deep and rich, and rolled over the whole room and seemed to fill every corner. Finn swallowed. "I am from the Scáthán. I mean, I'm from the kingdom of Loft, but I fell into the lake Scáthán, and now I am...well, I'm wherever I am now."

"I see," said the king. "Now that you have introduced yourself, I will introduce myself. I am the North Wind, the king of the Four Winds. This is my wife, the South Wind. My son at my right hand, with whom you have already spoken, is the West Wind, named Zephyr. And the one whom you know as 'Fleet'...he is my other son, and he is the East Wind. I believe he is out tending our clouds...or at least, he was."

Finn opened his mouth in surprise. Fleet was the East Wind? But why had he not wanted to come to see his family?

"My people are asking me about how the clouds disappeared," said the North Wind, gesturing to the people now on the outskirts of the throne room. "The clouds are under our protection. My people are being hurt because of the absence of the clouds. Do you know why they are gone?"

Now Finn had a choice.

He knew—he knew in his heart, and also because Una told him so—that *both* he and Fleet were to blame.

He understood now why Fleet had not wanted to come in to see his father. Fleet did not want to tell his father how he lost the clouds.

But Finn was also to blame, because he had also disobeyed his father and disturbed the waters of the Scáthán, and awoke the giant by trespassing on the giant's lake. But Finn did not want the North Wind to know that.

So Finn chose to do the wrong thing.

"Your son Fleet was tending his flock of clouds down by the Scáthán. I tried to tell him to move them away from the lake, but he did not listen to me. A huge giant made of clouds rose up out of the lake and whistled a song, and all the clouds from Fleet's flock and the whole sky followed him. He led them off somewhere across the lake."

The North Wind rumbled in anger. His wife whispered in his ear. But the North Wind could not see through lies so easily as Una could.

"My son has shamed me. He shall be punished."

And Finn felt that telling a lie that was not caught was much worse than telling one that was.

- 9 -

THE TRIALS OF
THE NORTH WIND

The North Wind stood up.

"My people," he said, addressing the whole room, "my son has shamed me. It is through his actions that the land is without clouds. For that reason, it rests on me to solve the problem of this giant—who must be the one who is called Iteoir Scamall, the Cloud Eater. He must be destroyed before he eats all the clouds, or the earth will dry up and crack and shatter."

He fell wearily onto his throne.

For the first time, Finn noticed how old he was. His beard was streaked with gray. He said in a quieter voice, that was still heard by all, "I do not think I will be able to destroy this giant, for he is very powerful. I would gladly give my life to this task, but I believe there are warriors here who would do justice and slay the monster."

His son, the West Wind, stood up. "I will go, Father!" he said.

A dozen other voices from the crowd—knights, all—also shouted that they would go. Finn noticed that the courtier with the nasally voice crossed his arms and wrinkled his nose, but said nothing.

"We must choose a champion," said the king. "And we must be swift. By tonight, we will determine who will go. I will devise three trials: the man who completes these trials will be our Champion, and he will slay the giant."

Finn watched all this in dismay. No one knew that *he* was to blame for bringing the giant out of the lake. He recalled the words that Una had said: *this weighs on your shoulders alone.* He could not just let someone else go and die in his stead.

But what was he to do?

"I have decided the first trial," said the king. "Who will participate in this competition?"

The king's son, Zephyr, stepped forward and said, "Me, sir." Several other knights clad in armor stepped forward as well, just as before.

"And me," said Finn. His voice seemed to be swallowed up by the large room.

The men smiled as if it were a joke. The courtier with the nasally voice snickered loudly.

The king looked at Finn and asked, "You are still a boy, and you would submit yourself for a man's job?"

Finn could not explain that he stepped forward because Una told him he must slay the giant. So he nodded, instead.

"Very well," said the king. "If you pass these trials, you, like anyone else here, will go to slay the giant. But these trials are cunning."

The king stood. "The first trial is this: let there be piles of grain, one pile for each contestant. Let there be many kinds of grain mixed together in these piles—rye, barley, and wheat. In one hour's time, the contestant must sort the grain into distinct piles. All the rye must be with rye, all the barley with barley, and so on."

It was done as the king said. Tall piles of mixed grain were made and each man was set before a pile. When the signal was given, each man—and Zephyr and Finn—threw themselves at the piles, sorting them out grain by grain.

At once, Finn saw that it was impossible. There was so much grain, and so many kinds, that there was no chance he could sort it into the correct piles in time. He could barely tell the difference between the rye, barley, and wheat. He stopped pawing in his pile, sat down, and wept.

He felt very alone—he had quarreled with Fleet, he had lied about his own role in angering the giant, and now he was going to fail the first trial. Was he ever going to get home?

Then he heard a very small voice. He looked around, then he put his ear to the ground.

"Do not mourn, boy. You spared us before, and now we will help you."

Finn smiled. He had forgotten about his ring that let him hear animals. It was the voice of the ant queen.

She called her subjects together and they came to help. They crawled into the pile and began sorting the grain—rye with rye, barley with barley, wheat with wheat. Before long, they had sorted the great pile down to the last grain.

Finn had completed the first trial. The crowd watching was surprised. Only a very few of the other men there completed sorting their piles by the end of the hour. Zephyr had also sorted his.

"Very well," said the North Wind. "I will now set the second trial for those who completed the first. You must bring me an apple from the Tree of Life in the Land of Youth. You must complete this task before the sun goes down."

Finn, of course, had no idea where the Tree of Life was. Neither did the knights. But Zephyr, the West Wind, smiled and took off running, leaping and bounding over the hills as only the West Wind could. Finn and the knights tried to follow him. But Finn could only run so far before he had to stop for breath. The other knights ran on after Zephyr, shedding armor as they went to reduce their weight.

Finn sat on a tree stump and put his face in his hands.

"How will I do this trial?" he said. "I can't run as fast as the men or the West Wind. I can follow the armor that they left behind; but there's no way I can get there and back before sundown. How can I get an apple from the Tree of Life in time?"

But someone overheard Finn's lament—the eagle he saved from the trap earlier. She had followed Finn to see how she could help him. The eagle soared in pursuit of Zephyr, and within an hour, she came back, holding an apple in her talons.

"Here is an apple from the Tree of Life," said the eagle, dropping a heavy, golden apple into Finn's hand. "My debt is repaid."

In delight, Finn took the apple to the North Wind, who received it with surprise, but also with a gracious smile. "Well done," he said simply. Finn smiled, and was grateful to Una for giving him the ring which let him understand and speak to the eagle.

Time wore on, and just before the sun set, Zephyr returned with an apple, equally as heavy and golden as Finn's. He put it in his father's hand.

"The knights are far behind," said Zephyr. "They could not pass the fiery river which runs around Tír na nÓg, the Land of Youth." He saw that his father already held another apple in his hand, and Zephyr also looked at Finn in surprise. Finn shrugged and smiled. Zephyr nodded at Finn as much as to say, *Well done.*

"So you two young men are the only ones who have completed the trial," said the North Wind. "Finn and Zephyr, the one who completes the last trial will be named Champion, and must go slay the giant. The last trial is this..." said the king, and took off his ring and threw it into the moat which surrounded the castle.

"The one who retrieves my ring will be Champion. The moat is deeper than you think. Good luck."

The boys looked at each other, and then in a moment both dove into the moat. It was deep, deeper than any other moat in the world, and neither of them could reach the bottom—indeed, there was no bottom, for the moat was connected to an underground river which sprung up from the heart of the earth, where a sea serpent named Oilliphéist[4] curled in deep sleep.

Finn opened his eyes under the water and tried to look for the glint of the king's ring. After a minute, his

---

4 Pronounced 'OHL-faysht.'

lungs burned, and he swam to the surface. He breathed deeply, and he dove again. This time he saw something.

You may remember how Finn had saved a fish that had been stuck in the reeds of a small stream. That stream fed into the very moat that Finn was in, and it was that very same fish that he saw swimming towards him underwater, carrying something shiny in its mouth. The fish swam right up to Finn and spat the king's ring into Finn's hand.

"Here is the king's ring," said the fish in a bubbly voice. "You saved me earlier, and now my debt is repaid." It swam away, its silver scales flashing back down to the depths of the moat.

Finn came back to the surface of the water and swam to the king. Zephyr came to the surface and followed behind Finn, defeated.

"Here is your ring, North Wind," said Finn.

And with that, the final trial was complete. Finn was the Champion.

- *10* -

A SHORT REST

The North Wind nodded. "Very well. Although the best warriors in the land, including my son, competed in these trials, you are the only one to complete them all. With that, I name you the Champion who must slay the giant."

"No hard feelings," said Zephyr, shaking Finn's hand firmly. "Well done on the tasks."

Finn wished he could rejoice, but a familiar feeling of dread seized him. He had completed the tasks, yes...but what about his true task? Defeating a giant seemed too impossible. His head spun. Why had he even completed the trials? Was he just going to get himself killed by a giant?

"We will help you to slay the giant," said the North Wind, gesturing to his wife and son, who was still dripping from his swim in the moat, "though we are but three of the four Winds. I fear my son Fleet will not be joining us, as he has betrayed us."

This made Finn wince.

"But as Champion, *you* are the one who must slay the giant. Is there anything you lack?"

Finn tried to think. *What does one need to slay a giant?* He would have liked some armor, but it would probably just slow him down. Anyway, armor wouldn't help much against a giant's fist. Ah yes... there *was* something he needed...

"I need a weapon," said Finn.

The North Wind smiled. "That I would be happy to provide you with. However, you have one at your feet."

Finn looked down. The ball of red yarn—the one that Una had given him—was at his feet.

"You mean this?" asked Finn, pointing at the ball of yarn.

"Yes. I know the one who gave you that, and she is very wise. She knows just what you need. At the right moment, when all seems lost, that yarn will change into the weapon you need."

Finn waited. But the North Wind did not give any more explanation.

"What will it turn into? A sword, or something?" said Finn.

The North Wind scratched his beard. "That I cannot tell you, because I do not know. There are some things that are beyond even me. However," said the king, pulling his own sword from his scabbard, "I can give you this. It is a sword of sharpness, quite deadly. It has slayed many monsters in its day on both sea and land." He turned the hilt of the sword to Finn.

Finn approached the throne and grabbed the hilt of the sword. To his embarrassment, when the king let go, the sword clattered to the floor. It was so heavy that Finn could barely lift it.

"Ah," said the king. "Then perhaps you must rely on the yarn."

Finn tried to look brave, but deep down he was annoyed. How was he supposed to fight a giant when he did not even know what weapon he would have? And what did the king mean, that the yarn would turn into the weapon he needed when all seemed lost?

"You may stay the night here. The coolness of the night will not dry up our land. But a morning without dew is unnatural, and soon the sun will dry out living things without mercy. You must go at first light. Rest here and prepare yourself for your battle."

Finn nodded, suddenly hungry. He had not eaten since he and Fleet had finished the food Una had given them before coming to the castle.

He was shown a guest room with a large bed and a window with a small balcony looking out to the east. Before long, food was delivered to his room—roast meat, bread, fresh butter and cheese, and a jug of what Finn guessed was wine. He was glad to be left alone, so he had a moment to think. But he was also growing more and more nervous in the silence.

He picked up the bread and cheese and went out on the balcony. After a day in the hot sun, the cool night breeze cheered him up a little.

He held in his hand the ball of yarn that had been leading him on his quest. *What is the secret here?* He supposed he should not be too surprised that the yarn could transform into something else. After all, it was certainly not a normal ball of yarn. It rolled along by itself and never seemed to grow smaller, even though it left a long, long trail behind that stretched back through the swamps, hills, and rivers Finn had crossed to get here, all the way back to Una's front door.

"Finn?" a voice said.

Finn spun around, nearly losing his balance and toppling off the balcony. He peered into his room. There was no one there.

"Finn, it's me, Fleet," the voice said. Finn turned, and he saw Fleet, the East Wind, next to him on the balcony.

THE FIGHT

"How did you get here?" said Finn.

Fleet shrugged and did not answer.

"Can you fly?" said Finn. Then he shook his head. "Wait, I have a more important question first. Why didn't you tell me you were the East Wind?"

Fleet sighed and looked over the balcony. He was sitting on top of the rail that encircled the balcony, dangling his feet over the edge. Finn would never have done that. His room was at least four stories up, and a fall would be deadly.

"So you met my family," said Fleet.

"Yes," said Finn.

"Were they mad?" asked Fleet.

Finn thought back to his conversation with the North Wind. He remembered how he had blamed

Fleet for angering the giant. He decided to change the subject.

"Why didn't you tell me you were the East Wind?" said Finn again.

Fleet kicked his feet over the edge of the rail. "I was embarrassed," he said. "My father is a king, the North Wind. And that makes me a prince, you see. My brother is older than me, and he will inherit the throne, but I'm still a prince. And I was embarrassed to be tending clouds like a common boy. That's why I didn't tell you."

This pricked at Finn's skin. He was, after all, a shepherd, and he thought that tending sheep was fun. With yet another pang of guilt, he remembered how he had failed his task to keep his father's sheep safe, and how he had led them to the forbidden Scáthán.

"Also," said Fleet, "I had taken the clouds to the Scáthán, the ancient lake. I knew I was not allowed to go there, but I went anyway. And...and I knew that the giant would be there. That's another reason why I didn't tell you."

Finn was taken aback. Fleet *knew* that the giant would be there? His surprise was quickly replaced by anger. How was Finn the one who was supposed to kill the giant, when Fleet had also disobeyed? When Fleet had known that the giant would be there? It was not fair.

Of course, Finn conveniently forgot at this moment that he had *also* been convinced that there was a giant at the Scáthán.

"So it's your fault!" said Finn. Fleet cringed and held up his hands, but Finn kept shouting. "Why on earth would you go to the lake if you knew the giant was there? You're the reason why the giant came out of the lake."

Fleet looked miserable. "Well, yes. But I didn't ask *you* to come flying out of the lake. I wanted to prove to my father that I could be a great warrior, and I thought...well, I thought if I slayed a giant, I wouldn't be tending clouds. But the giant was a bit bigger than I was expecting—"

"You're the reason I'm going to fight the giant tomorrow and get killed!" shouted Finn. "You were too scared to face your father and come to the castle. I completed the tasks that the king set, and that means I'm the Champion. And that means you're the reason I am going to die!"

Fleet's face began to turn red. "Hey, Una said you were to blame too. Didn't she say—"

"I don't care what Una said!" said Finn. "All she did was give us this stupid yarn and send us on a mission that would kill us. See what I care about what Una said!" Finn took the ball of yarn and threw it off the balcony. It fell out of sight into the dark evening light.

"I told your father the only reason the giant came was because you didn't listen to me when I said we should leave the lake!"

Finn stopped suddenly and put his hands to his mouth as if to stop the words from coming out. But they were already said.

Fleet's face turned even redder. Suddenly, an angry wind began to blow around him, whipping his hair in all directions. Finn remembered suddenly that this was no ordinary boy, but the East Wind.

"You said *what*?" said Fleet. "You told my father I was the only one to blame? You never said we should leave the lake. I can't believe you. Now my father will hate me, because of...because of your lies!"

The wind around Fleet grew and grew until Finn was sure he was going to be blown off. Without warning, Fleet leaped off the balcony, caught by his own winds, and glided down and out of sight into the darkness.

"Fleet!" Finn called. "Come back! Where are you going?"

But there was no answer.

Finn tried to stay angry, but after Fleet was gone, he could not keep it up. He sat on his bed and buried his face in his hands.

Now Finn was the most alone he had ever been. The only one with whom he had made friends in this land—Fleet—was gone. He had rejected Una's gift. And now the whole kingdom was relying on him to kill a giant.

It took him a long time to fall asleep that night.

- 12 -

SETTING OUT

"**M**ay you fell Iteoir Scamall, the Cloud Eater," said the North Wind.

It was early next morning, and the sun was not up yet. The North, South, and West Winds were all present.

The North Wind said, "The Cloud Eater has stripped our land of clouds, and now all living things thirst. The sun is merciless. The lakes and streams are drying up. The ground is as cracked as the lips of my people, for we lack water to drink. Go, Finn the Champion, and save us."

Finn's own lips were dry, but it was not because he was thirsty. He was nervous, and his heart was thumping loudly in his chest. "Yes sir," he said.

"Although we cannot leave the castle unguarded, we will help you," said the South Wind. Finn had not yet heard her speak. Her voice was gentle and warm. She smiled at him, and Finn felt a bit of his nervousness go away.

"Yes," said Zephyr. "Though I sure wish it was me going to fight the giant. I'm not sure if you know what you're doing."

The North Wind frowned at his son. "Do not speak to the Champion that way. He was chosen fairly, and you were given as much chance as he."

"Yes sir," said his son.

But Finn could not help but think that the Zephyr was right. He did not know what he was doing. All that he knew was that Una said he must be the one to defeat the giant, and that was what he would do.

"We will guide you to the giant, though we cannot go in person," said the South Wind. "Our thrones must stay occupied and we must care for our people. But we will send our winds with you, to help you reach the giant and to give you aid in battle as we can."

Finn bowed clumsily to the South Wind. "Thank you, Lady," he said.

Finn felt something bumping at his feet. He looked down and saw that the ball of yarn was impatiently rolling into him. He was surprised to see it back after he had thrown it away last night, but was glad it had returned to him. Apparently the gifts of Lady Una were harder to get rid of than he thought. The sun was just starting to peek over the mountains.

"I should go," said Finn.

The North Wind nodded. "Turn yourself east again, and we will take you to the giant's hiding place. The giant lives in the Scáthán, but he has no doubt taken the clouds to his hideaway in the valley into which the Scáthán drains."

Finn nodded and turned. He looked to the east. He could see the trail of red yarn that he had followed to get to the Castle of the Winds from Una's cottage. As he looked, he saw the ball of yarn start to roll away from him to the east and a little to the south, leaving a second trail of yarn alongside the first. Finn wondered again if the ball would ever run out of yarn.

"You are turned the right way. Follow Una's yarn. You will reach the Scáthán before the sun is at its highest point. The valley is beyond the Scáthán."

Finn nodded. His legs felt weak. He started walking.

"No, Champion. Run!" said the North Wind. Finn, startled, began to jog. "No," cried the North Wind, "run, boy, RUN!"

And Finn ran. As he did so, he felt the wind in his face, as you would if you set down this book and ran outside. But after a moment, the wind in Finn's face vanished. Finn was puzzled. He looked back over his shoulder.

The Winds and their castle was further away than Finn thought it would be. As he looked, the Winds each drew a deep breath, and blew in his direction. Suddenly, Finn felt the wind at his back. His speed picked up. He turned again to look where he was going so he did not lose his balance.

As Finn ran, he felt the gust of wind behind him growing and growing. He ran faster and faster, and the ground beside him blurred with his speed. The forest was already getting near, and still he ran faster.

Finn worried for a moment about running into a tree, but as he turned to avoid the first one, the winds helped him. They gave him a push here and a nudge there, and soon Finn was racing through the trees, faster than any boy had ever run before. He ducked branches and leaped streams, nearly flying along the ground. He felt weightless, as if he were flying. He outran the winds before him and outstripped the winds behind. He laughed for joy.

He nearly forgot what he was running to.

- *13* -

THE RUN

Everything around Finn was hard to recognize, he was going so fast. But he soon realized that there was something keeping up with him—in fact, going faster than he was.

The ball of yarn.

It raced in front of him, bumping along the ground and flying through the air. It unraveled as it went, leading a long, longer, longest line of red yarn behind it. Finn looked back, and saw the yarn running back through the trees, and thought of how long the line of yarn must be; it ran all the way from Una's front door, through the forest, to the entrance to the Castle of the Winds, and now back through the forest again. *It must be miles and miles long already,* he thought, and it was getting longer.

As Finn sped along his way, he had a chance to think. Now that the novelty of running with the Winds behind him was wearing off, he could think clearly about what he needed to do.

He felt the ring on his finger, and was reminded about Una. She had given him the ring so that he could understand creatures, which had helped him with the tasks he needed to complete to become Champion.

He thought back to everything Una had told him. She had told him that he must be the one to slay the giant. She had told him that the ball of yarn would "transform," whatever that meant. The North Wind had mentioned that, too. It must be important. Una had also said that the Winds would help him, and they were.

Once Finn exited the forest, he could see that the sun was rising before him. The light was so harsh that Finn had to squint his eyes nearly closed. He could rely on the Winds to guide him as he ran, so he did not worry about running into anything.

As the sun rose, Finn started to see why it was so terrible that the clouds had been taken. The ground under his feet was cracked and dry, and the grass was withering quickly. Plants drooped. The small streams that Finn had seen on his way to the Winds were completely dried up. There were a couple of small ponds, but even those had turned into shallow puddles.

As Finn ran by one of them, he saw that many animals were clustered about it, animals that should not be together—deer and hunting cats, rabbits and foxes, mice and owls. They were all quenching their thirst while they still could.

This made Finn realize that he *had* to kill the giant, or this world would die. And he would be responsible.

As Finn crested another hill, he realized that he must be getting near the Scáthán, the giant lake through which he had come to get to this land. He remembered that the North Wind had said the giant's hideaway was across the Scáthán, where it emptied into a valley. Finn did not know the way. Would he have to run around the lake? Which way would he go?

Finn came over another hill, and saw the Scáthán. He was running, running through the meadow where he had first met Fleet.

Fleet! Finn had nearly forgotten the fight that they had the night before. Finn had not seen him since then. *Well, if Fleet wants to abandon me to fight the giant alone,* thought Finn, *that is his problem.*

Finn told himself he would not think about it. But guilt is hard to remove from the mind.

And he remembered how Una had said that Fleet had his own part to play in fighting the giant...but maybe Una had been wrong.

But soon, all thoughts about Fleet vanished from Finn's mind. He was running through the meadow, getting closer and closer to the lake. Unlike some of the other ponds and streams that had dried up, the Scáthán still had plenty of water. It was certainly lower than it had been before, but not by much. And Finn was still running straight towards it.

"Wait, stop!" Finn yelled. He tried to stop running, but his feet kept going, and the Winds still blew behind him. He was heading straight for the water, and the Winds were not turning him to the right or to the left. He was going to fall in.

Finn leaped out over the water and for a moment ran in the air over it. Then he hit the surface.

But he did not break through.

The Winds kept pushing him forward and up, and he was running on the water. Spray flew up all around him. He looked back and saw the shore shrinking behind him as the Winds blew him over the Scáthán, over the deep, wide lake.

He couldn't see the other side, but he did not worry. If the Winds could help him run on the water, they could get him where he needed to go.

He looked down and laughed. A few feet ahead of him, the ball of yarn unraveled at an incredible speed, skipping over the waves and sending stinging droplets into his face.

- 14 -

THE GIANT'S
HIDEOUT

Finn soon discovered that the lake was not too wide. Although he could not see all the way across the Scáthán from the shore, soon after he ran over the lake, he saw mountains in the distance growing larger and larger. They rose up in spikes, like a circle of tall grass. That was where he was heading.

He got nearer and nearer. As he looked, he saw that the Scáthán went right up to the edge of the mountains. Only a small part of the Scáthán emptied into the valley, and it was a waterfall.

"I'd better not be going down that," said Finn. Thankfully, the ball of yarn skipping ahead of him did not seem to be taking him that way. Finn and the wind at his back followed it.

Instead, the yarn turned to the left, where the incline was not so steep and the base of the mountains turned into a grassy plain. As Finn neared the place where the Scáthán stopped and a sandy beach started, the wind at his back lessened. His legs and arms felt heavy, and his feet dipped below the water.

Soon, the wind at his back was spent, and he splashed his way through the last few steps to the beach. When he reached it, he collapsed, sucking in the sweet air and filling his burning lungs. He had not noticed how tired his legs were when he was running, but now they felt stiff and sore. He could have fallen asleep.

He felt something moving beneath him, wriggling back and forth. He yelled and rolled over onto his side.

"Oh, sorry," said Finn. He had accidentally laid down on the ball of red yarn and it had been trying to get out from under him. The yarn butted against his chest reprovingly. Finn watched from where he lay as the yarn rolled to the edge of the beach and stopped.

"Are you smaller than before?" said Finn. The ball, which must have rolled out miles and miles of yarn, was finally growing smaller. Before, it had been the size of Finn's head. Now it was closer to Finn's fist.

Finn rolled onto his back and closed his eyes, tired and spent. He put his arm over his eyes to shield them from the sun, and his forearm quickly felt hot under the sun's glare. After a moment, he felt the yarn bumping against his head. He shooed it away. It kept coming back and bumping into him insistently. *Why won't it let me rest?* Finn grabbed it and threw it away. Two moments later, it was back again.

"Fine," said Finn. He sat up. The yarn kept bumping at his leg. "Fine, fine, I'm getting up!"

Finn shakily got to his feet. His legs still burned, and he knew he needed to walk it off or they would get sore.

He hobbled around the beach. He glared at the ball of yarn. "There, I'm up now. Happy?" said Finn.

The ball of yarn, of course, said nothing back. But it did start rolling to the edge of the beach. Finn followed it.

Looking out from where the beach ended, Finn saw a valley pasture, hemmed in on either side by a mountain. On his right, the mountains that housed the giant and his hideaway loomed high over him. The peaks were jagged and sharp, and so steep that Finn wondered if he would ever be able to climb them.

A moment later, his mind was not on the peaks of the mountains, but on the giant stone resting at their base. It was still far away, but Finn thought it must be at least as large as the Castle of the Winds.

As he watched, the rock rolled, rolled to the side, opening up a tunnel in the cliffside. And out of the tunnel…

Finn had to shield his eyes, they were so bright in the sun. *Clouds!* Fluffy clouds, thin and wispy clouds, clouds shaped like hats and elephants and faces, clouds that whipped around, and others that moseyed on in slow motion—all these clouds spilled out of the cave in the mountains uncovered by the stone.

They scudded over the pasture, not going too far from the tunnel. In no time, the pasture was nearly covered with clouds. Finn remembered the flock of clouds which Fleet had kept; that was not even close to the number of clouds he saw now. It really was believable, now that he saw the vast number—the thousands and thousands of clouds—that the giant had taken all the clouds in the world.

Ah, the giant...

Finn saw him.

The figure of a giant made of rain, fog, and water crouched at the mouth of the tunnel. It was he who had removed the stone. As Finn watched, the giant shuffled through the tunnel and out into the open. He stood up to his full height. He was taller than the tallest tree Finn had ever seen.

Iteoir Scamall, the Cloud Eater. And Finn had to slay this giant.

UNEXPECTED FRIENDS

Finn quietly retreated back to the beach and sat down.

From this distance, the giant looked almost manageable, but Finn knew that the moment he got closer, the towering giant would be terrifying. He was so tall that Finn was not even sure the giant would notice if Finn walked right up to him.

Finn watched the clouds collect around the pasture. Apparently, like the sheep he had kept back in Loft, these clouds needed to graze and get some exercise.

Finn closed his eyes and turned over onto his back. What was he to do? Now that he was here, how was he going to defeat the giant?

Finn opened his eyes and sat up quickly. *The yarn!* Where was it? Finn saw the trail of yarn leaving the beach. Finn scrambled up to the end of the beach and looked at the pasture.

There was the ball of yarn, rolling steadily across the pasture. The clouds didn't seem to mind it, but drifted out of its way. The yarn was heading straight for the mouth of the tunnel that the giant had revealed when he pushed aside the rock.

Was that where he was supposed to go?

Finn could see the giant sitting beside the tunnel, resting his back against the cliff. He certainly was not asleep; Finn could see his thunderous eyes flashing as they swept the pasture, keeping watch over the clouds.

The ball of yarn kept steadily on pace to the tunnel. Finn was worried that the giant would notice it, but apparently the yarn was too, too small, and it passed into the tunnel and into the heart of the mountains without the giant's notice.

So Finn was supposed to get past the giant and into the tunnel. How was he supposed to manage that?

Maybe he could wait until the giant was done pasturing the clouds...but then the giant would cover the entrance with the stone, and there was no way Finn would be able to get past that.

Maybe he could sneak past the giant, like the ball of yarn did? But sneaking a ball of yarn past a giant was much easier than sneaking a boy...and Finn had read that giants could smell humans.

As Finn was wondering what to do, he realized that he could hear the low murmur of voices. It had been quiet at first, but now it grew louder. It seemed to be coming from the pasture. *Are there other people around?* he thought.

Finn poked his head over the lip of the beach again. The giant was too far away to see Finn. All Finn could see were the clouds, moving about in little packs back and forth, or standing still.

Finn could see no people, but he could still hear voices.

Then it struck him. He brought his hand up and stared at the ring that Una had given him. She had told him that he would be able to hear the voices of creatures. Finn didn't see any animals, but…

Could it be?

Clouds in this world were like sheep in his own. Could he really be hearing the voices of…clouds?

"Doesn't that giant know anything?" grumbled one of the voices.

Finn watched as four clouds drifted by him. Though clouds have no mouths, Finn thought the voice might be coming from a gnarled, gray cloud.

"We come out to pasture to drink the dew," continued the old cloud. "And he sends us out in the middle of the day!"

"To be fair," piped up another cloud, "he sent us out this morning, too. And we were out all day yesterday." This cloud was smaller than most of the others, was bright white, and had a higher voice.

"To fatten us up," said another cloud, morosely. This was a wispy cloud, and sounded miserable. "You saw the dinner he had last night. Gobbled up a whole flock. He just wants us to eat and eat and grow fat—"

"No fear for you, sir," said the small, young cloud. "You're still wispy as a baby's breath. But way older, obviously. Not as old as this guy, though."

"Hush," said the last cloud, and its voice was motherly. "Respect your elders."

The old, gnarled cloud grumbled something that Finn didn't catch.

Finn thought back to when he had heard the ants, and the eagle, and the fish. He was able to both understand and talk to those creatures, and so it must be the same for these clouds. Maybe he could ask them for advice or help. Finn got slowly to his feet and crept towards the clouds.

As he crested the hill and came into the meadow, the clouds stopped talking to each other, just like you might if you were talking to a group of friends and a stranger came and tried to join your conversation. Finn walked up to the group of four clouds to which he had been listening. He could not tell if the clouds were looking at him or not, but he cleared his throat, just to make sure he had their attention.

"Hello, my name is Finn," he said. "Can you help me?"

- 16 -

FINN MEETS
THE CLOUDS

"A human boy!" said the mother cloud.

"A boy? Why, he's tiny. He must be a baby human," said the young cloud.

"He can talk? Can he understand us? Maybe he's the giant's minion," said the wispy cloud.

"Let him speak," said the old cloud.

Finn cleared his throat again. It was so strange, hearing the voices from the clouds. At least when he was talking to the eagle, Finn could see its beak move. But the voices just seemed to come from out of the clouds.

There was a general hubbub around him of other clouds grazing and floating around, so he spoke up louder.

"No, I'm not a baby. I'm a boy. Yes, I can talk, and I can understand you. Can you understand me? I'm not the giant's minion. Actually, I'm the opposite. I'm here to slay the giant and rescue you and all the rest of the clouds."

Clouds, of course, cannot open their eyes, or stand suddenly, or grasp the speaker's hand, or otherwise do the kinds of things that a human would do if they heard welcome news. But what a cloud *can* do is shift around, undulating like smoke from a fire. This is just what the Wispy, the Old, and the Mother Cloud did (as Finn named them in his head). And if a cloud is young and spry enough, it will race around like it was tossed to and fro by a strong wind—and that is exactly what the Young Cloud did.

"Thank you, thank you, thank you, thank you!" cried the Young Cloud as it sped around Finn in circles. "That's just what we need. That giant needs some slaying. Sorry I called you a baby, but I haven't seen many humans."

"You are welcome here, dear," said the Mother Cloud. "It has been nearly two full days since the giant stole us from our pastures and our skies. We would like to go home, before…"

"…Before the giant consumes us," said the Wispy Cloud. "And he's been eating up plenty of us. Just you wait and see, I bet I'm next. I don't have much meat on my bones, though. I wouldn't make a very good meal."

Finn, of course, was reminded that the Wispy Cloud did not have *any* meat, nor any bones. But he knew what the Wispy Cloud meant; he wasn't big and fluffy like some other clouds. Finn wondered briefly what clouds tasted like, then realized that was a very impolite thought when in conversation with clouds, so he stopped thinking about it.

"And how, young human, do you intend to slay the giant?" said the Old Cloud. "His name is Iteoir Scamall, and he is a fearsome creature."

"Well, I'm not quite sure yet," said Finn.

At once, the Young Cloud, which had still been racing around and skipping over Finn's head, quieted down. "What do you mean, you don't know?" it asked.

"I mean what I said," said Finn, annoyed. "I'm not sure yet. But I'll figure it out."

"The other human who came here didn't know either," said the Wispy Cloud. "He just ran right up to the giant, said something to him, and was immediately snatched up."

"Other human?" asked Finn. "What do you mean? I thought I was the first person to come after you clouds. How many have come here so far?"

"Well, only one other human," said the Wispy Cloud. "And he was a young one—I would say about your height. I don't know; all humans look the same to me."

"What do you mean, only one other human?" said the Mother Cloud. "We know that human! He was our cloudherd. He had white hair."

Cloudherd? White hair? Finn knew immediately who it must be. His heart sank. What did they mean that the giant had snatched him up?

"Was it Fleet?" said Finn. "Did he tell you his name?"

"Oh, we don't know any names," said the Young Cloud. "You're the first human who is able to talk to us besides my owner. Her name is Una."

"This is her ring!" said Finn, raising his hand and showing the clouds. "That's how I know what you're saying."

"Did you steal the ring?" said the Wispy Cloud.

"No," said Finn. "Una gave it to me. She told me I have to defeat the giant."

"Well why didn't you say so in the first place?" said the Old Cloud. "We will help any friend of Una's."

"So where is Fleet?" said Finn. "Is he all right?

The clouds did not answer for a moment. Finally, the Mother Cloud said:

"The giant has taken him into his cave."

- 17 -

A PLAN IS HATCHED

"Hush...the giant stirs," said the Wispy Cloud.

Across the meadow, the giant stood up and stretched his arms over his head. It stood there for a moment, gazing around the meadow. Had he seen Finn? How was Finn going to hide? Finn looked wildly for a bush or a tree, but there was nothing.

"Here, you've got to hide!" said the Old Cloud.

"I know! But I don't see anything to hide behind," said Finn.

"Just float away towards that tree over there," said the Young Cloud.

"I can't float!"

"Oh, right," said the Young Cloud. "I forgot about you humans being so solid."

"I have an idea," said the Old Cloud. Right before the giant's eyes swept towards them, the Old Cloud floated right into Finn.

In a moment, Finn was completely covered by the gray, fluffy cloud. He immediately folded his arms and crouched down, shivering. The cold, frozen water around him immediately soaked him. He could not see outside the cloud, so he hoped that there was no way to see inside it. Finn crouched for a minute or two, waiting and praying that the giant could not see him. Then the Old Cloud moved off of him.

"Are you alright? The giant didn't seem to notice you," said the Mother Cloud to Finn, who was shivering with cold.

"That was way too close," said the Young Cloud.

"Well, it turned out alright this time," said the Mother Cloud. "But we need to be careful. The giant will be taking us clouds back into his cave pretty soon. And then...well..."

"Then he'll eat us," said the Wispy Cloud. "He eats clouds. Gobbles us right up like a hen pecking corn. I suppose your human friend will be alright, since the giant does not like eating humans. Well, he might not eat him, but he could starve your friend in a cage..."

"Quiet," said the Mother Cloud. "Don't scare the boy."

"Wait a moment," said Finn. He had been thinking all the while about how to get into the cave to rescue Finn and defeat the giant. "What were you just saying?"

"The giant will eat us and keep your friend there forever," said the Wispy Cloud.

"No, not about that. Did you say that the giant will be taking you inside his cave soon?"

"Yes," said the Old Cloud. "He takes us out a couple of times a day for an hour or so. We go out to graze in the meadow. Then he takes us back inside. We don't dare try to flee, for his terrible whistle calls us back. And he's sure to eat whoever tries to escape."

"Perfect!" said Finn.

"Well I don't see what's perfect about it," said the Wispy Cloud.

"Of course, it's not perfect that the giant eats you," said Finn. "That's horrible. What I meant was that I have an idea for how to get inside that cave."

"How?" asked the Young Cloud.

"I'll hide inside of one of you! When the giant calls you into his cave, you can go inside, and I'll walk along with you, and you can cover me up," said Finn. "It's like I'll be wearing a cloud disguise. The giant won't see me come in."

The clouds thought this was an excellent idea. They selected the Young Cloud to be the one to cover up Finn, since he was the brightest cloud and the hardest to see through. The cloud was very pleased to be selected for this task, and puffed himself up a bit—quite literally.

Before long, the giant rolled the great stone away from the mouth of his cave. He put his fingers up to his mouth and whistled, long and low. The clouds all started moving across the meadows, towards the tunnel.

The Young Cloud whispered, "Ready?"

Finn nodded, preparing himself for the cold, wet inside of the cloud. The Young Cloud moved over him, covering him up completely. As the cloud moved forward, so did Finn, shuffling and crouching to keep up.

"That tickles!" said the Young Cloud.

"Shhh," said the other clouds around them.

All of them—the Mother Cloud, the Wispy Cloud, the Young Cloud, and the Old Cloud, moved as a flock towards the mouth of the tunnel, with Finn in the very middle, inside the Young Cloud. They got closer and closer to the giant, and soon joined the group of clouds that were streaming into the tunnel.

In a moment, they passed right under the giant. Finn, of course, could not see what was going on outside of the cloud, but he could hear the giant's low whistling above him. He shuddered.

But the giant did not seem to notice the stowaway. And so it was that Finn entered the cave of Iteoir Scamall, the Cloud Eater.

18

A RIDDLE IN
THE DARK

For a moment, the inside of the cave was illuminated by the opening of the tunnel. Finn peered through the fluffy, white cloud, drenched and cold as he was. He was surprised—the cave was not very big, though it was very tall, and it did not go far back into the mountain. It was one big cavity in the stone, and Finn did not see any tunnels leading elsewhere. The entrance must be the only way in and out of the cave. The clouds all piled in from the outside, whispering with one another quietly and making room for each other.

"No you don't," Iteoir Scamall said behind Finn.

Finn huddled inside his cloud and his forehead broke out into a cold sweat. *Is this it?* Had the giant seen him? Finn peeked out of the cloud.

He saw Iteoir Scamall reaching down, looming over him. But he was not reaching towards Finn. Rather, the giant grabbed something by the mouth of the cave, scooping it up in his vast, misty hands. The giant walked a few steps into the cave—boom, boom, boom—and deposited what he had been holding on the ground.

Finn nearly shouted. There was Fleet! Wet, disheveled, and angry, but still alive. He must have been trying to sneak out of the cave and the giant had seen and stopped him.

Now the giant was back at the mouth of the cave and rolling the stone back over the doorway, with his back to Finn.

"Thank you," Finn said to the Young Cloud.

"Glad I could help. Good luck killing the giant," said the Young Cloud.

Finn quickly ran out from the cloud. The light was fading quickly with the mouth of the cave closing, and he had to get to Fleet before then. He ducked from cloud to cloud to make sure the giant could not see him, getting drenched anew every time he did. He muttered an apology to each cloud as he did this, because he didn't feel it was very polite to run through them without asking first, but he had to get to Fleet.

When he ducked into the cloud nearest to Fleet, Finn said, "Psst!"

Fleet whipped around. "Who said that?" he said.

Before Finn could say so much as "Shh," the giant rumbled, "No speaking, boy. You talk too much altogether. You make my head ache." The giant finished closing the door to the cave, and it was pitch dark.

"Fleet, it's me, Finn," whispered Finn. He could not see anything in the dark. "I'm here to help you."

"Finn?" said Fleet.

"Quick, get in here," said Finn.

"Into the cloud?"

"Right," said Finn.

Fleet bumped into Finn inside the cloud.

"It's cold in here," said Fleet. "And wet. How did you get in here?"

The giant growled.

"I can hear whispers," said Iteoir Scamall. "I can…" He sniffed. "I can smell you."

"Hey, that's rude," said Fleet. "Anyway, I'm the only one here."

"No," said the giant. "There is another."

Finn poked his head out of the cloud but could still see nothing.

He looked up and shuddered. No, not nothing… Finn could just see the giant's huge face, partially lit up by his lightning-laced eyes. They sparked and crackled with a reddish, yellow light, and lit up his nose and crooked mouth. The giant snarled and bared his teeth in the dim light. It seemed to Finn that there was nothing but the giant's glowing, angry face in a great sea of darkness.

"I do not know how you got in here," said the giant. "But you are very small. What are you? A mouse, a flea, a speck of dust?"

"I'm a boy," said Finn.

"Aha! I knew I could smell the hot, wet breathings of a boy. And...I remember you. I remember your smell. We have met before, when you tumbled into my lake. And what are you doing here now, trespasser?"

"I wanted to see the inside of your cave."

The giant laughed and said, "Well, you have seen the inside of my cave. By the end of the day, you will see the inside of my stomach! But before I catch and eat you, what is your name?"

"I'm...I'm nobody," said Finn, remembering Una's advice not to reveal his name. "And I thought you only ate clouds."

"Hmm, *Nobody*. An unusual name. Reveal yourself to me, Nobody, and you'll come to no harm," said the giant.

"What?" said Finn. "No. No way. You'll eat me or crunch me up or something."

Finn watched the giant's dim eyes flash around the cave. The giant was turning his head this way and that.

"I can hear you," said the giant, "but I do not know where you are in this echoing cave. I know you cannot escape, because I have rolled the stone to close the cave mouth. I could crush you if I stomped the earth all around this cave, but that would make me tired. I could wait until you starve, but that would take a long time. And I am not so patient."

The giant shifted and his glowing eyes dropped lower, and a loud thud told Finn that the giant had sat down. Even sitting down, the giant still towered over him. "So I propose," continued the giant, "That we play a game instead. If you win, I will release you from this cave."

"And if I lose?" said Finn. He wished his voice did not tremble.

"If you lose, you forfeit your life. Because I am generous, I will let you choose the game," said Iteoir Scamall.

Finn thought hard. In what game could he beat a giant? Certainly not arm wrestling.

"What will you do?" said Fleet.

Finn thought back to Una's advice. She had told him to not give the giant his name, which was why he had said his name was Nobody. What else was there? Ah, yes...she had also told him that the giant was fond of riddles.

"I propose a game of riddles," said Finn.

"A good choice. But because I am rather tired, I will only ask you one riddle. If you get this riddle right, I will let you go free."

Finn did not quite believe this, but he had no other choice. The stone covering the exit of the cave was too big, and the giant was the only one who could move it.

"Very well," Finn said. "Ask your riddle."

The giant thought for a moment. Then Finn watched as the dim light from the giant's eyes lit up a grin. In a low, sing-song voice, the giant said:

"I have no wings, yet I can fly.
I have no eyes, yet I can cry.
Darkness follows where I go,
Yet I am bright as driven snow."

The giant chuckled. "Now, what am I? Answer wisely, Nobody, for your life depends on it. And I suppose, if you get it wrong, I'll eat your friend too."

19

BACK INTO
THE LIGHT

Fleet said, "Eat me too? What do you mean? That's not fair."

"Fair is what I say it is," said the Cloud Eater. His eyes flared in the dark. They were dark red, the color of heat lighting. "And don't you help him, either. Fleet. The East Wind. The Rejected Wind, sent to tend the flocks like a common boy. You are a prince in name only. You hold no authority."

Fleet was quiet. Then he sobbed once, which he tried to hide by turning it into a cough, and was quiet again. Finn was glad that he could not see Fleet's face in the darkness.

"You told him your name?" said Finn.

"I didn't realize I shouldn't do that," said Fleet. "I said it when I challenged him. Then he said my name and commanded me to be still, and I froze up, like a chicken when it gets scared."

"Don't you remember that Una told us not to give him our names?" said Finn.

Fleet went quiet again. Then he said, "Well, I remember it *now*. Anyway, I wouldn't have come alone if you hadn't told my father those lies about me."

Finn winced. "Don't bring that up now. We have to get out of here. So back to the riddle—"

The giant rumbled like low thunder in the distance. "I'm waiting, Nobody," said Itcoir Scamall. "Of course, I know that is not your real name, or you would have revealed yourself when I commanded you to. I hear you whispering to your friend, though I do not know what you are saying. If you cheat and ask him for the answer, you have forfeited the game and I will eat you—though I prefer clouds for my dinner."

"No, no!" said Finn. "I'm not asking him anything. Let's see...I don't have wings, yet I can fly. Well, I suppose a balloon is like that."

"Is balloon your final guess?" said the giant.

"What on earth is a balloon?" said Fleet under his breath to Finn.

"No, that's not my guess," said Finn. He realized that there must not be balloons in this land. If there weren't balloons, how could the giant ask a riddle about them?

"Then guess. And no whispering," said the giant, "or I will stomp all around this cave and crush you where you stand."

Finn shuddered. He was still hidden inside his cloud, and it was still dark in the cave, so the giant could not see him. But a cloud would not be much protection from the giant's stomping feet.

Fleet was silent—there could be no help from him. *What doesn't have wings and can fly? And...oh, what was the rest of it?*

"Could you repeat it?"

Again in the sing-song voice, the giant said:

"I have no wings, yet I can fly.
I have no eyes, yet I can cry.
Darkness follows where I go,
Yet I am bright as driven snow."

Finn thought hard. What can cry without eyes? He thought about how the clouds were eating the dew off the grass when he first came to this world and met Fleet. Dew on grass was a bit like crying, but grass certainly couldn't fly. And what about the darkness and brightness?

Finn almost despaired. He had no idea how he would find the answer. He had never been good at riddles, and now his and Fleet's lives depended on one.

Hmm...the giant had said that Fleet could not help Finn solve the riddle. But what about help from other people? Finn remembered how the North Wind had told Finn that the winds would help him in the battle with the giant. Could this be what he meant?

"North Wind?" whispered Finn, so quietly that the giant could not hear him, so quietly that it was almost a thought. "South Wind? West Wind? Can you hear me?"

Finn waited, but heard nothing. Apparently the winds could only aid him in other ways.

The giant began to whistle his low whistle. The hair on Finn's arms and neck stood up. It was the first thing Finn had heard from the giant, back when Iteoir Scamall had risen out of the lake and first kidnapped the clouds.

After whistling a few eerie bars, the giant said, "I am nearly at the end of my patience, boy. Speak now or suffer and die."

Finn thought until he thought his brain would burst. He looked around himself, but the cave was still dark except for the giant's sparking eyes. Finn shivered and rubbed his arms. He was still very wet and cold hiding inside this cloud...

The clouds! Finn was surrounded by clouds that he could talk to because of Una's ring. He could ask them to help with the riddle, since the giant had only said that Fleet could not help Finn.

"Clouds?" said Finn.

"What was that?" the giant said. "Clouds? You said clouds?"

"No, I—" Finn started to say.

"Clouds, CLOUDS, CLOUDS, **CLOUDS!**" screamed the giant.

"I didn't mean to guess, I—" Finn started to say, and then he stopped. For he realized why the giant was angry: because "clouds" was the correct answer to the riddle!

What can fly without wings? Clouds.

How can clouds cry without eyes? Rain.

How does darkness follow clouds? In the shade that clouds bring.

And yet, clouds are bright as driven snow.

Iteoir Scamall stood up and screamed and stomped so hard that the whole cave shook. Finn listened to all this in some confusion. Where was the mysterious, deadly giant, the Cloud Eater? And when the giant started blubbering and whimpering and crying, Finn knew that the giant was throwing a tantrum like a little child.

"I won fair and square, giant," said Finn. "Now let us out."

The giant's weeping turned into moaning, and from moaning into sniffing, and from sniffing into silence.

"Well, giant?" said Finn. He wished his voice was stronger, for the darkness in the cave seemed to swallow it up.

"Very well," said the giant. "I will let you go free." The glowing eyes way up in the air disappeared as the giant turned and started to move the stone away from the opening to the cave.

"You don't really trust him, do you?" said Fleet.

"Of course not," said Finn. "But now that he's moved the stone, we can slip out. Quickly, hide in a cloud. Move while the giant is opening the cave!"

The boys were right. The giant, though he had just finished blubbering and acting like a fool, was still sly and wicked, and had planned to wait until the boys revealed themselves and to eat them up just when they thought they had gotten to safety. But the giant thought he had tricked the boys, and did not expect them to slip out while he was still rolling the stone aside.

And so the boys, under cover of clouds—the very thing that was the answer to the giant's riddle—were able to flee the giant's cave.

- *20* -

THE BATTLE
BEGINS

As the boys slipped out, even though they were as silent as a far up cloud on a sunny day, the giant bellowed, "I smell you, you rats, you little sacks of human jelly! I will crush you to paste!" And he began stomping all around the exit of the cave.

When the boys began running for the door, all of the other clouds streamed out, so that there was a huge mass of clouds like a cold waterfall flowing from the cave. The giant stomped and stomped, but since he could not see very well in the thick cloud cover, he could not stomp on the boys.

Darkness follows where I go, indeed, thought Finn smugly from the cool darkness of the inside of his cloud.

They came to the valley, and their clouds flew away. "Thank you!" called Finn.

"Good luck with the giant!" the clouds said back.

Finn grimaced and turned around. Behind them, the giant was still grunting and screaming and ripping the stone aside. They only had a few moments before the giant would come upon them in a rage. Finn looked around the valley quickly to get the lay of the land.

The sight Finn saw made his skin turn pale and a cry ripped from his throat.

For the land was dry, dry as driftwood cast far ashore. The ground was parched and cracked. The grass crackled pitifully under Finn's feet. The Scáthán was so low that a great plain stretched beyond where its beach lay, and small puddles of water and dead, stinking fish were all that was left. The sun beat down mercilessly.

Darkness follows where I go, thought Finn sadly. The clouds were not there to water the earth and give it shade.

Then Finn saw something streak across the valley from behind him, bouncing and rolling ahead of him. It was the red yarn. Finn had forgotten about it entirely. It was tiny, no bigger than a coin   it must be reaching the end of its tether. Finn looked back and saw the trail of red yarn left behind him, going in and out of the giant's cave.

And when Finn looked back, he also saw the giant, huge and awe-inspiring.

Iteoir Scamall, the Cloud Eater, steamed with rage. His cloudy visage trembled and roiled, like clouds before a tornado, and his whole body was green like the sky before a hurricane. Thick clouds swirled above his head, threatening a summer storm, and rain spattered from him in great droplets. Even in the fierce sunlight, his lighting eyes flashed like bonfires.

"I see you now, Nobody!" screamed the giant. "No one can save you—no more hiding in the dark, no more hiding in the clouds. I will eat you...no, I will crush you...no, I will seal you up in my cave until you wither away for lack of food and drink."

Finn and Fleet looked at each other and then down the hill at the unraveling ball of yarn racing down the valley.

"Last one there is a rotten egg," said Fleet.

"Last one there is *dead*," said Finn.

They ran down the hill, stumbling on the uneven ground. The giant bellowed again—no words this time, just a howl like an animal's, a howl that shook the ground—and chased after them.

A ways ahead of them, the ball of yarn stopped unrolling. In fact, it was no longer a ball at all; it had reached its end, right in the center of the giant's valley.

Fleet looked back. "We'll never make it," he said.

"Don't look back," said Finn, breathing hard.

"What do you expect will happen when we get to the end of the yarn?"

"Una said the yarn will change. It will change into something we need."

"That won't help us if we can't get there," said Fleet.

Finn panted and shook his head. The giant was right on their heels now.

"Time's up, little boys," said the giant. He gave a great stomp right behind them, and the earth quaked beneath him and threw the boys to the ground. Finn and Fleet rolled on their backs and watched the giant stoop down to grab them with his churning, cloudy hands.

Is this it? Was Una wrong?

Then the boys felt something ruffle their hair. The giant's arm was flung back as if a lasso had caught it and pulled it up and away from the boys. The giant staggered backwards.

Wind, powerful wind, blazed over the boys heads and knocked the giant backward. The boys were short enough that the wind flew over them, leaving them unharmed. But the giant was caught in the full blast of it.

"The North Wind!" shouted Finn.

"Dad!" said Fleet.

And the North Wind it was. After helping Finn run across the Scáthán to get to the giant's cavern, the

Winds had waited patiently in their castle, waiting to grant Finn the help he needed in the final battle with the giant.

Just as the giant was regaining his feet from the North Wind's blast, the South Wind blew as well. Now the giant was sandwiched between two fierce winds that blew together, trapping him. Yet the giant could still move sideways like a crab, and the giant bellowed and waved his arms threateningly. Then the West Wind picked up—*that must be Zephyr*, thought Finn—and one of the giant's arms was pinned to his side.

The three winds worked hard to keep the giant in check, but Iteoir Scamall could still move in one direction—the East. He braced himself against the Winds beating against him and stood his ground.

"Come on, Fleet!" said Finn. "Get up there, help them out. The giant is nearly trapped."

But Fleet did not move. At the sight of the Winds attacking the giant, he had shrunk down and turned pale.

"My father..." whispered Fleet. Finn could barely hear him over the giant's screams and the roaring wind.

"What?" said Finn.

"My father...I never apologized to him. I never said I was sorry for disobeying him. He's still angry with me. Anyway, what can I do? The giant's trapped there, there's nothing he can do."

"Fleet, Fleet," said Finn, shaking his friend. "Listen, Fleet, we need you. The giant won't be trapped with only three Winds. We need *all* of the winds to pin him down. See, he's reaching out that way, towards the East..."

The giant reached his free hand up to his mouth, and still fighting to stand among the fierce winds, put his fingers in his mouth and whistled, low and long.

ITEOIR SCAMALL, THE CLOUD EATER

The sound was so low and loud that it cut through the howling wind and shook Finn's chest. From all across the valley, clouds came pouring back, drawn by the song of the giant's whistle. The very clouds that had escaped the giant's cave were returning. Hordes and droves blanketed the valley in soft, white billows.

Finn watched in horror as the clouds approached the giant as if they were brainwashed, as if they were rats and the giant was the Pied Piper of Hamlin. The clouds drifted closer and closer to the giant. And even though the giant seemed to be trapped, he grinned so wickedly that Finn's back felt cold and his hands clammy.

The clouds drifted closer to the giant's face.

The giant stopped whistling, opened his mouth so wide that you would think he had no jaw, and inhaled.

Fluffy clouds, thin and wispy clouds, clouds shaped like hats and elephants and faces shot into the giant's mouth, disappearing into the giant's huge gullet without even a gulp. The boys watched helplessly as the clouds were eaten one after another.

"Is he...is the giant getting...bigger?" said Fleet.

Indeed, the giant, huge though he was, grew even bigger with every cloud he inhaled. Remember that the giant himself was already made of stormy clouds and water, and his eyes of lightning. So with each cloud the giant ate, he grew taller and fatter and stronger and bigger. It seemed to go on forever, there were so many clouds sucked up by the giant's great breath. The giant grew so tall that his head scraped the sky and the boys could hardly see his face, though they craned their necks straight up. And still the giant devoured more and more clouds.

"Quick," said Finn. "Let's get to the end of the yarn, while the giant's still busy."

"And I thought he was giant before..." said Fleet, looking at the giant towering above them miles and miles in the sky, taller than any mountain Finn had ever seen.

They ran the last few steps down the hill to where the yarn ended. Finn expected to see something, anything, that would hint at what he should do next. But all that was there was the slightly frayed end of the yarn.

He picked it up and waved it in the air. Nothing happened.

"Now what?" said Fleet. Finn shook his head. He didn't know what to do.

They turned back just in time to see the very last cloud be eaten by the giant. And that last cloud is what broke Finn's heart, for he recognized it as the Young Cloud who had hidden him and snuck him into the giant's cave. Though it tried to fight against the giant's breath, before long it lost its strength and was slowly dragged into his gaping maw.

The giant, still staggering under the winds beating against him, smacked his lips. The sound echoed all around the valley.

"HAH. Now there's nothing you can do about your precious clouds," said the giant.

The giant had been loud before, but it was nothing compared to now. The giant's words were heard as far as the Castle of the Winds, where the North, South, and West Winds stood, and all the people who had sought shelter there.

"They are in me. They are me. And now I will crush you."

The boys could see that the Winds were losing their strength, for the giant began struggling towards them, one labored step at a time. The Winds could not hold him back forever.

Finn turned to look at his friend. "Fleet," he said, "I can't think of anything we can do. The yarn hasn't changed into anything useful, like we thought it would. And I'm afraid we might not make it. But I wanted to say this first. I'm sorry I blamed you. I'm sorry I told your father that it was your fault that the giant stole the clouds. I'm sorry I did not take responsibility for my own actions. In fact, I have never told you this, but my own father told me never to go to the Scáthán, but I disobeyed him. I'm sorry about that, too."

Fleet looked at his friend. "Finn, apology accepted."

And at that moment, the yarn in Finn's hand grew heavy. Finn gripped it in surprise and looked down. He had once been holding the frayed end of red thread. Now he held a thick handle wrapped in leather which fit his hand perfectly. He watched as the red yarn turned into a skillfully braided strip of leather, until there was no thread left. All along the ground where the yarn had once lain was a thick leather coil. Finn stared at it for a moment before he realized what it must be.

It was a whip.

A whip as long as the red yarn had been.

A whip a hundred miles long.

And Finn realized what he must do.

"Fleet, can I ask you a favor?" he said.

"Of course," said Fleet, who was staring at the whip in amazement.

"Keep that giant still for me, would you?"

Fleet flashed his old, mischievous grin. "Glad to," he said.

Fleet ran to the side of the giant that was still free and unhampered by wind. The giant tried to swing at Fleet, but he was so tall that Fleet could easily avoid the giant's swing. Finn watched as Fleet stood a safe distance from the giant, took a deep breath, and blew it out toward the giant.

The giant staggered back from him, struck by a great wind from Fleet. Finn saw all the other Winds pick up, as if they knew they were united in strength and were giving their last efforts to hold the giant still.

So it was that the giant, Iteoir Scamall, the Cloud Eater, was pinned on all sides by the four Winds.

Finn raised the whip as high over his head as he could. He could lift a bit of the whip in the air, but the rest of it lay heavy on the ground behind him. He felt ridiculous, but knew that this was the right thing to do. With a massive heave, he cast the whip over his shoulder as if throwing a baseball, then drew it back over his head to crack it.

Up, up, up it went. The whip curved high over Finn's head, as if it were a gigantic snake poised to strike. On it went, further than Finn would have ever felt possible. He guessed that the winds must be helping the whip along.

He heard a heavy whisper behind him, and when he looked, he saw the whip traveling along the ground behind him, following the path that the red ball of yarn had traveled.

Finn thought back to where the very first thread had been laid…

- 22 -

THE JOURNEY
OF THE WHIP

Far, far away from Finn, in the land called Ceann Amhàin, where there was just one of everything and a mysterious lady with red hair lived in a little house on a little hill, something moved.

Una had watched the red yarn which had lain on the entryway of her house for the last day. She had seen it turn into a whip, as she knew it would. Then she waited to see what was to be seen.

In a moment, the whip was gone. It flew down the path that the two boys had traveled, when she had given Finn the ring and the ball of yarn, and they had gone off to the Castle of the Winds.

Una smiled as it went. She looked at the sky, and waited.

Still the whip went on.

On and on it went, zipping through trees and over streams, up hills and down valleys, following everywhere the ball of yarn had gone. The yarn had led the boys to every place they needed to go, which meant that it was miles and miles long.

At the Castle of the Winds, where the yarn had stopped for a moment, the whip snaked through the grass, moving at such speed that the ground smoked and sputtered.

The courtiers and people who had come to seek shelter at the castle during the drought watched the whip. Many had come to the castle as soon as the giant had taken the clouds, and many more had arrived in the last half hour, for when Iteoir Scamall had eaten all the clouds and grew to a terrifying height, he could be seen and heard through all the land.

The Winds, however, were inside the castle. They were seated on their thrones, concentrated on the battle that Finn was having with the giant. The East Wind's throne, of course, was empty, for Fleet was with Finn at the battle.

The West Wind's eyes were closed, and his hands clenched the armrests of his throne. His mother, the South Wind, furrowed her brow, and it was a wonder to see her soft and kind face so changed. Her eyes also were closed in concentration. The North Wind, however, sat with his eyes open and aflame, his hand on his ruling scepter, staring to the east where the giant stood.

The people outside the castle watched as the tip of the whip screamed past, and all was suddenly quiet. The ground was blackened and charred all along where it had gone. And to this day, the place through the forest and over hill and vale where the red thread traveled and the whip left its mark, is called Finn's Road.

And still the whip went on.

It was coming to the end of its journey. Now the tip of the whip was traveling where Finn had run that very morning, when he was pushed along by the Winds. It zipped along, heading toward the Scáthán, where it had all begun, and where Finn and the yarn had run across on water.

The whip flew above the water that had not yet dried up. Where it touched the water, spray flew up, and the puddles boiled around it.

And so the whip came across the Scáthán.

Still the whip went on.

The whip finally came to the valley where Finn had met the clouds. It climbed up the beach, into the meadow, and then sped towards the tunnel of the giant. It was in and out of the cave in a moment, before it hurtled to the place where Finn stood.

At last, the tip of the whip left the ground. But it still had to curve up and up towards the giant, heading towards his very forehead.

23

CRACK!

Finn kept his eyes fixed on the giant's head.
The giant was struggling against the fierce
Winds, but they held him firmly in place.

The whip curved over Finn's head like a great
question mark, and he was its point. He watched as
the tip of the whip sped up and up. He could barely
see it, the giant was so tall, but he knew that the whip
was heading directly for the giant's forehead.

Any moment now, it would strike the giant.
And then—

Crack!

—the crack of the whip was so loud—

Crack!

—that its echoes—

Crack!

—were heard—

Crack!

—throughout the land.

Crack!

Finn's eardrums throbbed with the sound. The whip was falling to the ground all around him, its job done, but Finn kept his eyes fixed on the giant.

The great Cloud Eater teetered back and forth, rocking on his thick legs. A low moan rumbled out of its mouth. Then...

The giant fell.

Back he fell, his great arms waving in the air. The giant was so tall and great, that it took a long time for him to fall. Finn sat down in the grass—surrounded as he was by the whip—and watched the fall of the giant.

When the giant's head finally met the ground, Finn expected there to be a great crash, and he clapped his hands over his ears.

But there was no sound when the body of the giant hit the ground. Instead, it burst into a great shower and mist. Nothing was crushed by the fall of the giant, for the giant was nothing but water.

The waters flew high, high up in the air. Much of it crystallized in the cold air, and Finn laughed to watch it   for he saw clouds, the very same clouds that the giant had eaten, form in the cold air and zip around the sky. Because of Una's ring, Finn could hear them yelling and cheering at the giant's defeat.

Only some of the water turned into clouds—much of it became rain, and it was the heaviest rain that the land had ever seen. For a half-minute, the rain fell, drenching everything. The giant was so big and his fall so great that the whole world was watered again.

Finn was drenched with water.

The Scáthán's water rose to its usual height.

The people and the Winds in their castle cheered at the rain.

Una smiled in her house as she heard the water patter on her roof.

All across the land, streams and rivers and lakes and ponds that had dried up were suddenly whole again.

Finally, the rain stopped.

And you know what happens after a great rain and the sun shines in the still damp air?

A rainbow appears.

This was the biggest rain that the land had ever seen, so it was followed by the greatest, most vibrant rainbow ever to exist. It had the reddest red, like summer strawberries. Orange as dying fall leaves. Yellow as the sun itself, and the daffodils that soak it up. Green as cat eyes. Blue like a winter ocean. Purple as the crocuses and violets that burst from the ground after a spring rain. The band was so bright and so strong that it lasted a day and a night, and shone even in the light of the moon.

24

THE FEAST

Of course, a great celebration was held in honor of Finn when Iteoir Scamall, the Cloud Eater, was killed.

It took place outside the Castle of the Winds. Huge tents were set up, striped with blue and white and gold. The very best of food was there: fish cooked to perfection, stuffed goose, roast oxen, bowls of mashed potatoes dripping with butter, strawberries and fresh cream, cheese and bread and olives, cakes and pies. And to drink, there was wine, blackberry cordial, wassail, and—of course—plenty of water for everyone.

Many peoples were there from all over the land. They wore bright clothes, but not the kinds that are frilly and impractical. No, they wore the kinds of clothes they could dance in, for dancing there was. The very best musicians were there, and played on lutes and pipes and drums, and many more instruments that Finn did not recognize.

Finn sat in the place of honor, with Fleet right next to him. He sat with the Winds. He spoke little, but laughed and listened much, for the Winds had many wonderful stories to tell and Finn wished to remember them all.

Fleet was happy to be back with his family, and they were glad to have him back. The night before, Fleet had a long conversation with his father, and their fellowship was restored. He often tousled Fleet's hair and proclaimed loudly that he had "caused a lot of trouble" for him, but there was a twinkle in his eye when he said this. Zephyr constantly asked questions about the fight with the giant and wanted every last detail. Fleet's mother spoke little but smiled much.

But at one point in the festivities, towards the evening when there was more silence and lower voices, and everyone was content and sleepy, the North Wind looked at Finn and said, "Champion, I see you are downcast. What is troubling you?"

Finn looked up at the king, and saw that his face, which was still regal and full of authority, looked at him kindly. Finn said, "Sir, I am grateful for the honor you have all shown me. And I am very glad that the giant is gone. But I am the one at fault for disturbing the giant in the first place. None of this would have happened if I had obeyed my father and not gone to the Scáthán. Then the Cloud Eater would not have woken up, and the clouds would not have been taken, and the land would not have dried up. So why am I still honored?"

The North Wind laughed and said, "You are right. You are at fault in stirring up the giant, and no one here denies that. But it is no little thing to take on responsibility for one's own mistakes. And you have done just that. You were the one to wake the giant, yes. But you were also the one to pursue and slay him."

"But I didn't do it on my own. I had help from all kinds of people—from you, and Fleet, and all the Winds, and Una, and the clouds when I came to the giant's hideout," said Finn, and he sighed, for he remembered the clouds that were eaten by the giant.

"Ah," said the North Wind. "And that is another wonderful thing. We are not left to deal with the consequences of our sins on our own. If we were, we would never overcome them. But help is sent, and we are not alone, and for that you must be grateful."

"Thank you," said Finn, and they spoke no more of it.

All great feasts come to an end. By this time, Finn wanted to return home and see his father and family—he had been gone for nearly three days now. It was decided that he should go back before the sun fully set. Fleet quickly volunteered to walk back with him to the Scáthán so that Finn could return home.

Finn said his goodbyes to the Winds, and he and Fleet started back.

They spoke easily all the way back, laughing and recounting their adventures. Soon they came back to Una's house, for Finn had to return the ring.

As they walked up the little hill towards Una's house, Finn suddenly stopped and laughed. For at the top of the hill, just like Una had said so long ago, there was a little cloud—her own little cloud that she tended.

And it was not just any cloud. It was the Young Cloud who had helped Finn sneak into the giant's hideout. As soon as the cloud saw Finn, it raced toward them and flew around them, cheering with joy at seeing him again.

"I thought you were dead!" said Finn. "I saw the giant eat you and all the rest of the clouds!"

"Oh, no," said the Young Cloud. "The giant was very gluttonous, and he swallowed all of us up whole. So when he fell and burst apart, we came out of him unharmed."

Finn said, "So that means that you and the Mother Cloud and the Wispy Cloud and the Old Cloud all made it out alive?"

"Hmm," said the Young Cloud. "Do you mean the clouds that you met before you entered the giant's cave? Those are not their names. But yes, we are all alive."

"What are your names?" said Finn.

Then the Young Cloud said several names, but Finn could not quite make them out, for they were cloud names, and impossible for humans to say.

"I see," said Finn, though of course he did not. "I will try to remember your names. I will try to remember everything here. But I need to speak to Lady Una."

Finn and Fleet knocked on the door of the house and were bid to enter.

Una sat inside, weaving at a loom. Her hands moved back and forth in a whirl, and the shuttle flashed in her hand.

"Welcome back," said Una. Her smile was warm as hot chocolate and a hearth.

"Lady Una, thank you for everything you've done for us," said Finn. "We would have been lost a hundred times over without your red thread. I'm sorry I couldn't return it to you—I left it in the giant's valley. Though, it isn't a thread anymore, but a great whip a hundred miles long."

Una nodded. "It will find its way back to me," she said.

"Remembering your advice was the only way I could have gotten out of the giant's cave," said Finn. "And one of your greatest gifts," said Finn, taking the ring off his finger, "was this. I could understand the animals that helped me with the tasks. I could speak to the clouds, who helped me sneak into the giant's cave."

Finn handed it over to Una wistfully. He would miss being able to talk to animals. Una took it from him graciously and put it back on her own finger.

"But most of all..." said Finn slowly.

"Most of all?" said Una.

"Most of all, you helped me to understand to take responsibility for my mistakes. I could not just shift the blame and place it on others. I needed to be obedient and make up for my wrongs. Of course, I couldn't do it alone," said Finn, putting his arm around Fleet's shoulder. Fleet laughed as if he were a bit embarrassed, but he didn't shove Finn's arm off.

"Well done, Finn and Fleet," said Una. "But Finn, you still have unfinished business." She was silent again.

Finn thought for a moment. Then he said, "I need to talk to my father. I started all this mess when I disobeyed him and went to the Scáthán. I need to make it right."

"Good," said Una. "Your way home is open. You entered as a thief through the back door, but you may leave as a prince through the front. You may return the same way you arrived."

"Lady," said Finn. "There is one thing I forgot to mention. It feels like it happened so long ago, but I think it is important. When I first came through the lake, I felt as if someone was grabbing me by the back of the neck and pulling me through. I don't believe it was the giant. The hand was human-sized, and it had long fingernails." Finn grimaced at the memory.

Una's face was troubled, and she said, "A person with long fingernails...I do not know what that may be. There are creatures and people in this land besides giants who are driven by evil, and may have been seeking to do you harm. Was there anything else amiss?"

Finn thought hard. Fleet, who had been listening intently, said, "Finn, do you remember that voice?"

"Ah!" said Finn, snapping his fingers, "I had forgotten about it. When we first disturbed the giant and he was deciding how to deal with us, a voice seemed to whisper in his ear, even though we did not see anyone around. I couldn't hear what it was saying, but I think it persuaded the giant to do something. Or maybe not to do something."

"A voice. A clawed hand..." said Una. "It would have to be a powerful creature to pull you from your world into our own. I will need to think about this.

Why would someone seek to bring you to our world and goad the giant? It is possible that there are greater things afoot…"

They were all silent for a moment.

Then Finn asked, "Lady Una, will I be pulled by that hand when I go through the lake this time? It was a terrible feeling."

Una was silent for a moment, her head bowed slightly. Then she smiled and looked at Finn, taking him by the hand. Hers was warm and gentle. "Rest assured that with my blessing, you will travel safely and easily to your own land. Perhaps I will see you again, Finn. And Fleet, you are welcome anytime."

The boys took their leave, and left the Lady of Ceann Amhàin.

- 25 -

HOME AGAIN

Finn and Fleet were quiet for the rest of the way back, and spoke little. But it was not the sullen silence that had plagued their journey a few days ago. It was a contented silence, and touched by a little sadness. They knew a goodbye was coming soon.

The Scáthán was not far from Una's house, and in a moment they were on its banks. The sun was setting over the trees behind them, and the Scáthán was tinged pink.

"Well, this is it," said Finn.

"Yes," said Fleet.

They stared into the waters of the Scáthán.

"Do you think you'll come back?" said Fleet.

"I'm not sure," said Finn. "Una said she might see me again. Last time I came through, it was an accident.

I was more like an intruder than a guest. But maybe I'll be invited back. This place is beautiful."

And indeed it was. Sunset fire gleamed off the lake, night water-birds were waking up and skimming over its surface for the evening midges, and the plants and flowers were vibrant and blooming after the great shower from the giant's fall.

"And I have friends here," added Finn.

"Yes," said Fleet, smiling his crooked smile. "Though you have a funny way of making friends—bursting through a lake, waking up and slaying a giant..."

They laughed.

"Goodbye," said Finn.

"See you later, maybe," said Fleet.

Finn jumped off the bank into the Scathan.

Down he fell. He closed his eyes and waited to splash into the water and feel its icy touch.

But there was no splash. And he felt no water.

No clawed hand pulled him through.

Rather, he felt as if a pleasant, scented breeze had washed over and through him as he floated down into warm darkness. He felt as if a soft hand—Una's hand—was leading him lightly by the wrist...

....

Finn opened his eyes. He was lying on the bank of the Scáthán. He turned his head, and—no, was that a cloud? Had he come back home, or was he still there?

Then—

Baa-a-a-a-a!

ABOUT THE AUTHOR

Nathan Miller lives in the golden wheat hills of the Pacific Northwest with his wife Elli, their two young giant-slayers, and a ball python named Butterscotch. When he's not reading old stories, he enjoys looking for creepy crawlies and eating homemade biscuits and gravy. For more information, please visit **nateandellimiller.com**.

If this book tickled your noggin

and you find yourself feeling a tad

nosey about other available titles

and forthcoming releases, visit

nogginnose.com

NOGGINNOSE

PRESS

a curious name for curiouser books